Praise for *USA TODAY* bestselling author Caro Carson

*Winner of a RITA® Award
for* A Texas Rescue Christmas

"[Caro] Carson's romance is a humorous and heartfelt page-turner from the get-go. Her funny, genuinely touching and vibrant narrative sets the perfect pace with just a touch of Texas twang."
—*RT Book Reviews* on *The Bachelor Doctor's Bride*

"This romance is a real trauma twister, dealing with delicate social and political issues. The narrative flows and the characters shine."
—*RT Book Reviews* on *Doctor, Soldier, Daddy*

"This is a Christmastime hit and will be a great read for anyone who needs a little bit of Christmas magic, a good ol' Texas cowboy and a princess who decides she wants to be real."
—*HarlequinJunkie.com* on *A Texas Rescue Christmas*

"One-liners rule in this sensational Texas Rescue tale where playful banter is foreplay to a tender love story."
—*RT Book Reviews* on *Following Doctor's Orders*

Dear Reader,

Love at first sight is one of the most romantic phrases. Do you believe in it? The hero of this book swears it happened to him and his new bride. Captain Tom Cross meets and marries Captain Helen Pallas the same day. The wedding-crazy city of Las Vegas makes that possible.

But...

What if one person forgets that day ever happened? Then you have *The Captains' Vegas Vows*, and a marriage that faces the hardest of tests before the ink is dry on the marriage license.

This book was inspired by a true event. While I was in the army, a friend fell in love on a summer assignment. After just a few wonderful weeks, her new boyfriend fell seriously ill. When he woke in the hospital, he couldn't remember the last few weeks of his life—which meant he didn't remember falling in love with my friend. In real life, they went their separate ways when the assignment ended. My friend moved on to meet and marry her husband, have lovely children and a successful career—a happily-ever-after she is enjoying to this day.

But...

That story has always stayed with me. My imagination has run wild with the possibilities over the years, until I just had to write *The Captains' Vegas Vows*. I hope you enjoy it!

I love to hear what you think. You can email me privately through my website at www.carocarson.com, or post a comment on Facebook. I'm at www.Facebook.com/authorcarocarson.

Cheers,

Caro Carson

The Captains' Vegas Vows

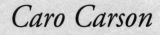

Caro Carson

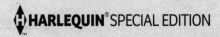

HARLEQUIN® SPECIAL EDITION

Recycling programs
for this product may
not exist in your area.

ISBN-13: 978-1-335-46607-5

The Captains' Vegas Vows

Copyright © 2018 by Caroline Phipps

Printed in U.S.A.

Despite a no-nonsense background as a West Point graduate, army officer and Fortune 100 sales executive, **Caro Carson** has always treasured the happily-ever-after of a good romance novel. As a RITA® Award–winning Harlequin author, Caro is delighted to be living her own happily-ever-after with her husband and two children in Florida, a location that has saved the coaster-loving theme-park fanatic a fortune on plane tickets.

Visit the Author Profile page
at Harlequin.com for more titles.

This book is dedicated to the men and women of the real 720th Military Police Battalion at Fort Hood, Texas, and the 89th Military Police Brigade, in which I was privileged to serve, once upon a time. Thank you for continuing to assist, protect and defend the soldiers of the United States Army.

Chapter One

The first time she woke up, she was surrounded by diamonds and gold.

It was magical. It was right.

She smiled because she wasn't awake enough to laugh, then she slipped back into sleep.

The second time she woke up, she blinked in the night, awake enough this time to be aware of the sounds of a city beyond the room. Beside the bed, diamonds and gold reflected the lights that filtered in, color after color, as if there were a party outside, turning the diamonds into a kaleidoscope. Since her pillow was very soft under her cheek, and since her whole body felt wonderfully soft and relaxed, too, she fell back asleep.

The third time she woke up, the diamonds and gold were brilliantly lit by the steady, white light of the sun.

She stared at the bedside table, an entire piece of furniture made of gold. The clear base of the lamp upon it was filled with diamonds. Why would anyone fill a lamp with diamonds?

Her brain began to grind into gear. The table had to be brass. The diamonds had to be crystals. That was only logical; no one had the money to fill a lamp with diamonds.

She wasn't in her own bed—also logical. Of course she wasn't in her own bed, because she'd moved out of her lonely house in Seattle and was driving 2,500 miles to Texas, staying in a different hotel in a different state each night.

The trip wasn't exciting, just routine, because she was an officer in the US Army, and she had no choice but to move when the army told her to move—which, so far, had been five times in the past eight years. Each move had been predictable, from her initial training course in Missouri to her first assignment at Fort Bragg, North Carolina, from there to a deployment overseas, then back to Bragg. Her promotion to captain had been followed by another training course in Missouri, followed by two years as a company commander at Joint Base Lewis-McChord, just south of Seattle.

Everything occurred in the proper order on the proper timeline. Every time she was moved, she filled her car with suitcases, duffel bags and a reliable little toaster oven. The army stored her furniture, delivering it when they left her in one place for more than half a year. When it was time for the next move, the army sent workers to box it all up and store it again.

Because her life was full of duty, predictable duty, and because every mile she traveled was the shortest distance between two army-ordered points, and perhaps because it was nearly her thirtieth birthday (although thirty wasn't any more significant than any other age—really, it wasn't), she had decided to add some excitement, taken a detour and stopped for the night in Las Vegas.

Vegas, baby.

Oh, my God, I'm in Vegas.

Captain Helen Pallas bolted upright in the bed and realized immediately that not only was she in Vegas, she was nude, and she had a horrific headache. She pressed one hand to the side of her head and yanked the white sheet up to her neck to cover her breasts, which caused a little avalanche of rose petals to cascade down the sheet to her lap.

She was sitting in a bed—a gold bed—full of rose petals, a thousand of them under her legs, even between her toes. She stopped pressing her palm into the side of her pain-filled head and instead ruffled her newly bobbed hair, dislodging more petals. They fluttered over her shoulders and down her spine to land with a soft tickle behind her bare backside.

Roses are always going to make me think of sex now.

Helen clutched the sheet more tightly. Was that a real memory or had it been a dream?

"Roses are always going to make me think of sex now."

"Is that a bad thing?" he murmured in her ear, laughter always underlying that deep bass. They'd just been laughing; they were going to laugh again.

She snuggled into him a little more deeply, loving the way they fit together, spooning on their sides with her bare back against his warm chest, loving the strength in his arm as he kept her securely against his body.

"Red roses are supposed to represent true love," she said. *"Romance. Not the hottest, wildest night of sex in your life."*

"True love and romance." He scooped up a handful of rose petals and pressed them to her breast, cupping them to her skin. When he slid his thumb slowly over the curve of her breast, the velvet of a petal created a fragrant friction. *"Like this?"*

She shifted in response, sliding her legs together, feeling the pleasant abrasion of his masculine legs against her smooth ones, enjoying the casual intimacy of their bare feet touching. "No, I mean a wholesome, pure kind of love. You're using roses to make me think of hot sex again. Right this second—yes, just like that. That's sexy."

He slid the handful of rose petals down her body, their softness exquisite, her skin more sensitive than she'd known it could be. Everything with him was better than she'd known it could be. She smiled even as she shivered when his hand stopped just below her belly button.

He kissed her shoulder, scraped his teeth along it gently, then a little lick, another kiss. "But the roses came after I pledged myself to you. So did the sex."

He slid the petals lower still, down to the most sensitive part of her body, and gently pressed them in a firm circle, or two, or three. She tried to breathe deeply, but anticipation had her panting. He let go of the petals to slip his hand under her thigh, to lift her

leg and position her a little differently. A little better.
"First, we promised true love."

She ached with desire as she listened to his voice.

"They showered us with rose petals after." He
held her in place with a strong hand on her hip, and
stroked into her, joining their bodies. They sucked in
their breaths, in unison, at the sensation. *"Love first,
then roses."* Another smooth stroke, his velvet friction inside her, the velvet roses all around her. *"So
rose-scented sex, hot sex, all the wild nights in our
future—"* his body inside hers, his hands on her skin,
his words in her heart *"—started with pure, wholesome, true love. Wouldn't you agree—"*

Stroke.

"—Mrs.—"

Stroke.

"—Cross?"

"Oh, my God." Helen whispered the words in a
panic. Her head throbbed. Her mouth was dry. She
was married.

Was she?

She grabbed a fistful of her hair and tugged gently,
but she couldn't remember anything else. The night
wasn't even a blur in her memory; it just wasn't there
at all. Yet here she was, naked in a bed, panicking on
a pile of petals.

Mrs. Cross?

No. Please no. I would never—

She wasn't Mrs. Anyone. She was Captain Helen
Pallas, and she was never going to change that for a
man, never again, no way, no how. Her divorce had
been final just two days ago. She'd gotten the court
papers, gotten her army orders, gotten on the highway.

She let go of her hair and slowly held out her left hand. Diamonds and gold surrounded her ring finger, glittering in the morning light as she trembled.

She'd gotten married.

A doorbell rang. Helen snatched her hand back to clutch the sheet more tightly around her neck. This bedroom was part of a suite, because the door was open a few inches and she could see a little bit of a Liberace-worthy candelabra and a shiny satin sofa in the next room. It sounded like a door in that living room opened, then men's voices murmured. She looked frantically around the floor, but not one piece of clothing cluttered the carpet. She kept the sheet clutched to her neck with one hand as she stood and started jerking the rest of the sheet off the bed with her other hand, petals fluttering in the air like startled butterflies.

"Will that be all, sir?" asked one male voice.

"Yes."

Helen stopped moving. That one syllable, *yes*, was spoken in a voice so deep, she knew it was the man who had said other syllables, words like *sex* and *love*, words that had made her melt.

Dark hair—he'd had dark hair. And he was big, not just tall but broad shouldered, hard muscled and—and tan skin, and—

And—

She could only hiss at herself for not knowing who had put a ring on her finger. She yanked the giant California-king-size sheet free and started wrapping it around herself. The sheet was white, but the red petals had left pink splotches everywhere. She'd heard of sprinkling rose petals on a bed, of course, but she'd never heard that the luxurious, romantic gesture caused stains. No one mentioned that part.

Of course it ruined the sheets. What romantic gesture didn't turn into a disaster?

"Thank you, sir." The more-talkative man sounded so cheerful, Helen could only assume he'd gotten a generous tip. "Congratulations again to you both. Just call us if you need anything else, anything else at all."

Helen held her breath, but the deep voice she listened for didn't make any answer. The outer door opened and shut again. With the sheet wrapped around her chest and securely tucked under her arms, she braced herself for the coming confrontation. She stood still, practically at attention, and waited for the man who'd said *yes* to come into the bedroom to talk to her, his new bride.

A bride. *Good God, Helen, what is wrong with you?*

She'd been through this once already, and once had been one time too many. If this Mr. Cross was any kind of decent human being, he'd know—he must know—that she'd been drunk last night, and he wouldn't dream of holding her to any drunken promises she might have made.

She didn't want to rehash a night she could barely recall with a man she could barely recall. She was thirsty. Her stomach was unsettled. She needed breakfast. If this Mr. Cross would let her eat and then let her go and pretend nothing had ever happened, that would make him Mr. Right.

She heard some rustling about in the next room and swallowed down her sense of…anticipation? Surely not. Panic? She didn't like to think of herself as someone who panicked. She was an army officer. She could handle whoever came through that bedroom door.

Nobody did. Instead, a shower started running. The hotel suite must be very big, with more than one bathroom, because the bathroom attached to this bedroom was empty. Somewhere beyond this bedroom, her groom was taking a shower, something apparently more important than checking on his new wife.

Stop expecting anything else. Ever. From anyone.

The fake gold and fake diamonds in the bedroom furniture were ridiculous. The rose petals were impractical and staining, and the gold-and-diamond band on her finger was—well, it was returnable, surely. She just needed to go tell her supposed groom that he could return it, and if any kind of legal document existed, they'd have to undo that, too. Yes, she'd just tell…what was his name?

"Mrs.—"

Stroke.

"—Cross."

Stroke.

Cross. Tom Cross. Not Thomas, but Tom. It was coming back to her.

Helen kept facing the bedroom door, but as she looked at the opulent bed out of the corner of her eye, something else in her brain stirred. Something significant had happened on that bed. Sex, the wildest sex of her life, had taken place there, and it had been… She held her breath again, willing her brain to work.

Fragments, just little bits and pieces of memory, ran through her mind, but they were enough. It wasn't that the sex had been wild. It hadn't been a *Kama Sutra* re-enactment or anything, but it had been…unrestrained.

She'd been unrestrained, fearlessly surrendering to him, letting him set the pace, letting him have his fill of her. She'd felt so safe, so *relaxed*, she could do anything, say anything, have anything from him she wanted. Over and over again, she'd responded to his touch, to that deep voice in her ear—oh, what exactly had he said?

Her skin felt warm. Her heart was beating hard. She'd loved whatever he said, she knew that much, because her body was responding—*please yes more*—to her fractured, incomplete memories.

Arousal was useless right now. Helen couldn't crawl back in that bed and wait for the man to get out of the shower, even if she wanted to. Which she didn't. She couldn't—she needed to extricate herself from this situation and get back on the road to Fort Hood. She had to report to her new unit by noon tomorrow. There were no clocks in this room, but judging by the sun, it was full morning, and she still had at least eighteen hours to drive. She was *not* going to report late to her new post because of a one-night stand. That wasn't acceptable to the army. It wasn't acceptable to her. Captain Pallas would never be so unreliable. Never so unprofessional.

How many times had her ex-husband mocked her for that?

Once, Helen, just once, would it kill you to be late to formation when I want to have sex with my wife? Not every chick in the military is as uptight as you are, thank God.

The headache that had started to recede came back in full force, but Helen couldn't let a little thing like physical pain stop her. She had orders to obey.

She'd taken an oath for the army long before she'd made any vows with this Tom Cross. Unlike a husband, the army would never change its mind. Legally, she had to be in Texas by 1200 hours tomorrow, or she would be AWOL—absent without leave.

A real commitment like that made decisions easy. She would bid farewell to this Tom Cross, give him back his ring and hit the road. There was no other option.

The sound of the running water stopped. Helen marched out the bedroom door, head throbbing. The sheet trailed behind her like a train, a mockery of a wedding gown. This wasn't a real marriage, anyway, thank goodness. She wouldn't survive another goodbye like the one that had ended her real marriage. This was just a one-night stand. She'd never had a one-night stand before, but how hard could it be to say goodbye to a stranger?

There was no dark-haired man in the gilded living room. Instead, there was breakfast for two, a beautiful table set with linens and silverware and more roses, white and pale pink and pastel yellow, forming delicate bouquets in mini crystal vases.

Roses are always going to make me think of sex with you.

Not just sex, but sex *with you*. She'd forgotten that part. There'd been something special about him.

Or at least she'd thought so while under the influence—obviously, or she wouldn't be here right now, staring at a wedding breakfast while her stomach churned and her mouth felt like it was full of cotton.

She walked up to the table, gathering her train around her. Silver domes were keeping the plates warm. Nothing about this beautiful table said one-night stand. It was her idea of a real wedding breakfast, every detail of it lovely, as if the man who'd ordered it had wanted her to have the best. She could be the pampered bride of the perfect man.

Tears stung her eyes.

She could be a sucker. Any man could play the prince for twenty-four hours. Her ex-husband had pulled it off for several months, actually, before the two years of misery had begun. This Vegas guy was being charming for *one meal*. Helen wasn't going to get all mushy because some man she'd frolicked with in a king-size bed was being charming for one meal.

She ignored the sparkle of the ring on her finger as she grabbed a crystal goblet and chugged orange juice like it was water from a canteen during a twelve-mile road march.

Better. She plunked the empty goblet down and lifted a silver dome. The heavenly scent of bacon made her mouth water. She took one bite before reaching for the carafe of coffee. It would help her headache and keep her awake for the eighteen-hour drive that lay ahead of her. She held the strip of bacon between her teeth, so she could use two hands to pour.

"Good morning, beautiful."

That deep bass—Helen whirled around, cup in one hand, carafe in the other, bacon dangling from her teeth.

Good God, he was gorgeous.

I slept with that?

Mr. Cross had short, thick, black hair, yet his eyes were an arresting, brilliant blue. He leaned more toward rugged than pretty, with the great bone structure that could sell expensive watches or yachts in a magazine for men who wanted to be more manly. But no—it wasn't that rugged handsomeness that would make men want to be like him. It was the way he carried himself, the way he stood before her with only a towel wrapped around his waist, unselfconscious despite being half-naked, that really knocked her out. Confidence was sexy to her. A man with an athletic body and a handsome face who seemed in charge, in control—and comfortable to be so—was sexy as hell.

I slept with that!

Well, damn, she was impressed with herself.

He smiled at her, a real smile that made the corners of his eyes crinkle and revealed some perfectly straight, perfectly white teeth. Where had she found this man?

She didn't realize she was smiling back as he walked across the room toward her—confidently, of course—until he took the dangling strip of bacon from her mouth. Her smile faded as she looked into those blue eyes. He was really looking at her. Only her. All his attention was on her.

"Good morning," he said again. He tossed the bacon onto the table, slid his arms around her and kissed her.

She melted instantly, going completely boneless in some kind of Pavlovian response that required no conscious thought at all. The cup and saucer slid from her fingers to hit the floor with a crash, the carafe landed with a thud in the tangled train of sheets, but she wouldn't fall, not as long as he held her in his strong arms. She made a little sound, a whimper of longing, a pant of excitement, and he broke off the kiss to cup the back of her head in his hand and whisper over her lips. "I thought I dreamed you. You're real."

They stared at each other a moment, then he was kissing her again and she couldn't keep her eyes open. She couldn't keep any thought in her head, except to know she could surrender, she could lose herself and let go, and she'd be safe and happy and a part of him. She was glad when his hands untucked the sheet, grateful when he nudged her back toward the couch, where they fell together as they pushed yards of sheets and one plush towel out of their way. She was greedy to touch him once more, to feel again all that strength and power and male grace. She wanted it all, forever.

Do you take this man to be your lawfully wedded husband?

I do.

His body filled hers completely, and the whole world became just the two of them and the way they felt, the way they made each other feel, the way they moved together. They whispered their amazement to each other in syllables that never became full words—*ah, oh, ess*—and in words that never became sentences—*my, you, there*. They climaxed together, then lay still, catching their breaths in silence.

I now pronounce you man and wife.

Mrs. Cross started to cry.

Chapter Two

The woman beneath him started to laugh—or at least for a second, Tom thought she was laughing, because they'd laughed together last night.

This was different.

"Helen?"

She had one hand over her eyes, her ring hand. The sight of that diamond and gold band choked him up, too, a sob of gratitude sticking in his throat, gratitude that he'd finally met the woman he'd dreamed of. His wife. *His wife.*

His wife was crying.

"Hey, Helen. What's going on?" His voice came out a little more husky than normal, emotion making his throat tight, because she was wonderful, and he didn't want this wonderful woman to be upset. About anything. Ever.

She took in a shivery breath, one he felt through her whole body and his, joined as they were. He kissed her hand and she lifted it away. Her eyes were closed and her lashes were wet, although no tears had spilled over. He brushed her hair away from her cheek, savoring their physical closeness, skin against skin, and he waited. His wife often paused before speaking, but she always answered him. He loved that about her. He would never have to cajole, beg or plead with her to talk to him. She was the last woman in the world who'd resort to giving him the silent treatment.

Helen opened her eyes, those beautiful warm brown eyes, and looked at him the way she'd been looking at him since their eyes had first met across a crowded casino.

"I…" She cleared her throat.

He waited.

"I can't believe I did this."

"This?" He raised one eyebrow as he looked down at her. "This seems to be what happens whenever we're in the same room. We've been doing *this* all night."

He smiled gently at Mrs. Tom Cross. It was an emotional morning. Crying was a normal reaction at weddings. He kissed the corner of her eye before a tear of joy could slip away.

The slight salt on his lips did something to him. To his heart. He felt it expand, like a lion stretching in the sun, full and satisfied. Content—he felt supremely content, heading into the rest of his life as a married man.

"All night?" She looked away, and pressed her fingertips into her forehead, like someone trying to think hard. "Yes, of course we have."

"Of course," he echoed her, and shifted some of his weight off her. "It was our wedding night."

She shielded her eyes with her hand as if looking at him was as painful as looking into the sun. "It really was?"

He frowned. She hadn't meant that to sound like a question, surely.

She held her hand out a little way to look at her wedding ring. "This is really…real?"

Another emotion tried to crawl up the back of his throat, threatening his contentment. He swallowed it down and kissed the tip of her nose. "Is that question really real?"

She didn't smile.

He suddenly couldn't, either. "You're serious. You don't remember?"

She looked away again, concentrating, but after a moment, she shook her head. "No."

Alarm tried to choke him, but he beat it down. This was temporary. They'd had a lot to drink and not a lot of sleep. Helen would remember.

He'd tell her. "We picked out that ring together. It nearly made us miss getting the marriage license. Vegas may be 24/7, but even their government offices close at some point. We got there in the nick of time, just before the stroke of midnight, Cinderella."

She didn't smile. She didn't even hold his gaze.

"You don't remember buying the ring?" Alarm, panic—he swallowed them down, but damn, they made it hard to speak.

She looked at him, eyes bright with unshed tears.

He spoke as gently as possible. "What do you remember?"

"Um…just…"

Helen took another shivery breath beneath him. He made sure most of his weight was on his forearms, tensing his arms, his shoulders. It didn't change anything; her breathing was still too shallow, too rapid.

He could barely breathe at all.

Tom remembered that she'd loved her dress. She'd been so happy with what she'd called the perfect dress. He wanted her to remember happiness. "Don't you remember your dress?"

She shook her head.

"The ceremony?"

"No."

Our vows? You said you loved me, and you would love me forever. You promised.

Even if he hadn't been choking on this sense of dread, he wouldn't have said those words out loud. Begging someone to love him never worked. He'd learned that early in life.

"Tell me what you remember." His voice was quiet and gruff. It didn't sound like his voice, nothing like the soldier he was, even as he gave her a command: "Tell me."

"Just…this. Kind of."

"This," he repeated impatiently. "Sex?"

She nodded.

She remembered the sex. That was all.

"I'm sorry," she whispered.

His heart simply stopped beating.

She placed her palm over his heart, but only to push against him, bracing herself as she shifted a bit like she was going to get up.

He was still inside her. What was the proper etiquette for this? Was he supposed to beg her pardon and withdraw? What was the damned etiquette?

He pulled out of her body, breaking their connection, feeling his heart tear out of his chest at the same time. The misery on Helen's face tore at him, as well. Regardless of what she remembered, she was still his wife, and it was still true that he didn't want her to be upset, ever.

He wouldn't allow it. He was a warrior, an officer in the US Army, trained to move forward, not to give up. He wouldn't surrender to this heartbreak. He'd fight to ease his wife's current pain. He could fix this.

He caressed her cheek once more with his thumb. "If you didn't remember our wedding, then what was this? Don't say it was just sex. There's more to us than that. Why did you just make love to me?"

"I don't know." As she looked up at him, the tears in her eyes finally spilled over, running into her hair. "I just…when you kissed me… I guess I remembered something."

He kissed her again. If this made her remember, this is what he'd gladly do. He kissed his wife, *until death do us part, forever and ever, amen*.

She melted under his kiss, opening her mouth, kissing him, until she gasped—no, she cried—until more tears ran into her hair.

"Helen, Helen." He dried the tear tracks with the pad of his thumb. "Everything's going to be okay."

"I need… I just need…"

He waited. She would tell him, talk to him, share her innermost thoughts with him.

"I need my clothes." She pushed against his chest

again, sat up, then grabbed a fistful of the rose-stained sheet and pulled it around herself. "I need my clothes."

That kiss had been a start. She remembered something. She was just hungover. Some juice and water, some food—everything would be okay, just as he'd said.

"I think you need food," he said.

"I need my clothes."

He'd heard that tone of voice from her before, flat and uncompromising. It was how she spoke about her first marriage. About her ex-husband. Now she was using it with him.

He forced himself to smile. "Your suitcase is still in your car. You ran up here with nothing but the dress you had on. And me. We were all we needed."

She seemed embarrassed by that. When he stood, she was definitely embarrassed, blushing and dropping her gaze.

He turned away from her. He picked up a silver platter from among the decorative roses he'd ordered as part of her first breakfast as his wife. "Food. How about some bacon?"

"How about a towel?" She held out the plush towel while keeping her face turned away.

First she made love to him, now she couldn't look at him? No—first she'd stood in a wedding chapel and told everyone that he was everything to her, and now she couldn't look at him.

Tom knew that routine. Dad putting a proud arm around his shoulders, introducing him as his son to other men. Dad refusing to even look at him after Tom had lost the hundred-meter dash. Dad driving away from the track, forcing Tom to run home, unwanted.

Dad telling him he ought to thank him for the extra conditioning that he'd so clearly required. *Thanks, Dad*, he'd said sarcastically.

Tom tossed the platter back onto the table. Helen had pulled that towel off him, and now she needed to avert her eyes? He grabbed the towel out of her hand and retied it around his waist, sarcastically, if one could make a movement sarcastic. "Better?"

Helen's face crumpled, just crumpled into tears, and the old wall that had so quickly gone up around his heart crumbled. She bowed her head.

Tom dropped to one knee by the sofa and ducked his head a little, trying to see her face. "I'm sorry. This is a rough way to start our first day. But I'm here with you, and you're with me, and we'll get through it. Some coffee, some food, a shower. You'll feel better, and you'll remember, dream girl, you'll remember."

Her head snapped up and she gasped.

"What is it?" he asked.

"Dream girl…" She remembered. He could see it in her face for one shining second.

Then it was gone.

Helen stood, clutching her sheet, and backed away from him. "I'm not your dream girl. I'm not anyone's dream girl. I'm very sorry, but I don't know you. You're a stranger to me."

Tom dragged himself to his feet, as if every inch of his six-foot-two frame was made of lead.

Helen took another step back. "I realize last night… last night must have been different than this, but please believe me, I don't remember."

Tom tightened the knot on his towel, but it didn't

matter. Nothing he did was going to make her treat him as anything other than a stranger.

She held her palm up like a police officer telling him to stop. "I need my clothes, and I need to leave."

He held both hands up, an innocent man who wasn't putting up any fight.

She kept backing toward the bedroom. Not a cop, then. More like a beautiful princess retreating into her fortress. "Do you know what time it is? Is it noon?"

"Nearly two o'clock." He dropped his hands.

She looked stunned for one second, then she started gathering up the trailing sheet quickly. "I have to go. I have to be somewhere by noon tomorrow—"

"I know. Fort Hood."

Surprise made her hesitate for a moment.

My God, she really remembers nothing, nothing we said, nothing we planned.

It hurt.

Pain was an old enemy. Tom had learned to deal with it before he'd learned to drive a car. *Thanks, Dad.* Helen wasn't locked in a fortress—his heart was. It had been for a long time, untouchable, invulnerable.

Until Vegas.

Until Helen Pallas. She was the one person who'd found her way to his side of the wall. She'd wanted to stay there, forever, the two of them safe and happy together, so certain they'd never feel pain in their little world for two that he'd let the wall disintegrate. With Helen by his side, he didn't need to be on guard. Hopes wouldn't get dashed. Love would never be withheld in chilling silence.

Please remember. "I was here this weekend because I'd flown in for a friend's wedding. Vegas was the closest airport to the resort they married at, across the state line, in Utah. Then I came back to Vegas, and I saw you. Everything changed. We decided I'd cancel my return ticket and drive with you to Fort Hood instead." *Please remember.*

She took another step back. "That's crazy. This isn't some kind of honeymoon road trip. I've got orders to report to Fort Hood. I'm an army officer."

"I know you are, Helen."

Her eyes widened a fraction in surprise. She clutched the sheet more tightly to her chest. "I'm traveling on orders. It's at least an eighteen-hour drive, and I've only got twenty-two hours at the most to make it. I'll barely have time to stop for gas and food."

"That makes it more important for me to go with you. We can take shifts driving through the night. It will be safer." Her safety mattered, because he remembered everything, and she was his wife. He'd sworn to love, honor, cherish her. *You swore the same to me.*

Helen sounded angry. "This isn't some sexy Vegas game. This is real. The real United States Army, real orders, real clock ticking. You are a stranger to me. There is no way I'm going to spend eighteen hours in my own car with a perfect stranger."

A stranger. Him.

The wall got higher, stronger. It felt so familiar. *Thanks, Dad. You don't want me for a son? Then I don't want you for a father.*

She abruptly stopped retreating. "Let me be clear. No means no."

He laughed at that, knowing he sounded obnoxious. "I assure you, I can take no for an answer. It hasn't been part of your vocabulary."

"It is now. The answer is no. Do not cancel your plane ticket to wherever you were going. Do not cancel whatever plans you had. Don't change anything for me. Just tell me where my clothes are, and I'll be gone from your life."

Don't go. The wall around his heart felt the same, but his heart was no longer the same within it. With every beat, he wanted his wife.

She did not want him.

"Your dress is in the shower." His words were stiff. Unemotional.

She frowned. "Why is it— Never mind." The rosy flush reappeared across her cheekbones, across her chest.

He stayed where he was, towel around his waist, arms crossed over his chest. He was made of stone. He was the wall. Stone didn't bleed. Walls didn't beg.

Then Helen returned wearing her wedding dress, and he wanted to howl in pain.

She dropped the sandals she carried and started pushing her toes into the sparkling straps as she finger-combed her hair, a whirlwind of action in a long elegant gown.

"You need to slow down." His voice was astoundingly even. Then again, why should it waver? The worst had happened. He'd fallen in love and had that love rejected. Everything from this point on was inconsequential. "Ten minutes won't make a difference. Eat."

"I should have left hours ago." She gave up on her hair and dropped her hands with a sigh. "Look, Tom, you seem like a really nice man. I'm sure we had a really good night, but you can count yourself lucky that

I have to go. This would have been a giant mistake. I'm not wife material."

"Too late. Literally, you are wife material."

That gave her pause. "Is there…*paperwork*?"

"The license was signed and kept by the chapel. They file it with the county. In two weeks, the official certificate will arrive in the mail."

"I can't believe I did this to myself." The misery on her face infused her whole body. She seemed to fold in on herself, looking too small for the white column gown she'd worn with such confidence. "How could I do this to myself?"

Damn it. His heart wouldn't stay behind any wall. He was supposed to care about his wife. He did care about her.

He took one step closer to her, but she stopped him with a raised hand. She raised her chin, too. "No—I'll take care of everything. A divorce. An annulment. I don't know, but I'll get a lawyer when I get to Texas, and I'll get this all straightened out, I promise."

That wasn't the promise she'd made the night before. It wasn't the promise he wanted. He refolded his arms across his bare chest and didn't get any closer.

"So, um, Tom, could you write your number down for me? For the lawyer? Quickly? I'm running so late."

"It's already in your phone." They'd gotten married. Of course they'd exchanged all of this kind of information. "I have your number."

She ran her hands down the sides of her dress. "No pockets. Do you…do you have my phone?"

He nodded toward a shining brass credenza, where both their phones had been tossed. His wallet was there, as well. He picked it up. "I have your driver's license and your military ID."

"Oh." She laughed nervously. "That would have been bad, to leave without those." She took the cards with one hand and stuck her other hand out to shake. "I guess this is goodbye, then. I'll be in touch as soon as I find out what to do legally."

He let her stand with her hand outstretched. They'd just made love on the sofa. Now she expected him to shake her hand like a stranger?

It was enough to put that final stone in the wall—until he saw that the hand she offered him was trembling. The wall came tumbling down again, that quickly. His heart demanded that he take care of his precious bride. *For better or for worse...*

Helen dropped her hand. Her attempt at a smile only made the sadness in her eyes more obvious. "Goodbye, Tom." She skirted around him to head for the door.

"Stop." He caught her with a hand on her arm. "You're not going anywhere until you eat."

She looked at his hand on her upper arm, then raised her eyes to his. Dark eyes. Angry eyes. "Or else what?"

"Or else I won't let you leave."

The loathing on her face was not how he'd ever dreamed she'd look at him. He was being a pompous jerk, making rules for her like her ex-husband had.

He wasn't her ex-husband. Not yet.

She didn't need to be given orders. She needed help. He let go of her and walked past the sofa to pick up the house phone. The operator greeted him by name. Obsequiousness came with the penthouse suite. "Good morning, Mr. Cross."

"I need the valet to bring the car around as quickly

as possible. It's urgent." He turned back to Helen and gestured toward the table with the telephone receiver before he dropped it back in its cradle. "They'll have the car up in five minutes. You might as well eat."

She glared at him a moment longer, but apparently common sense won out, because she turned to the table and grabbed a croissant. She stuffed some bacon slices in it, then sloshed some orange juice into a glass and chugged it down.

With the croissant in her hand, she sketched him a sarcastic salute. "Goodbye, Mr. Cross."

His bride walked out the door.

Chapter Three

Captain Tom Cross rapped on the frame of the brigade commander's open office door. Two firm knocks: firm because he was a captain in the US Army, as the double black bars on his camouflage uniform attested, but only two knocks because the brigade commander was a colonel, three ranks higher than captain. It would be disrespectful to bang on the man's office door demandingly.

"Come in." Colonel Oscar Reed looked up from his paperwork. "Captain Cross. What brings you to my office on a Monday morning?"

"Do you have a moment, sir?" *So I can tell you how much I screwed up?*

"Come in. Give me a minute." He returned to his paperwork, signed his name and tossed his pen down.

Tom stood in front of the desk, if not quite at the

position of attention, then close enough. The formality of military courtesy fit his emotional state, or lack of it. Since approximately 1400 hours yesterday—two in the afternoon, when his wife of mere hours had walked out on him—he'd felt nothing. He was made of stone.

"Welcome back," Colonel Reed said. "How was Utah? Friend's wedding, wasn't it? How'd it go?"

"Yes, sir. He's married now."

"Well, yeah, that happens on wedding weekends." The colonel started to chuckle. When Tom didn't join him, he sat back and kept his too-sharp gaze on Tom. "You're standing there pretty formally. I take it you're here on official business."

"Yes, sir."

"Why didn't I hear from Colonel Stephens that you'd be coming?"

Lieutenant Colonel Stephens was the battalion commander. Lieutenant colonels wore a silver oak leaf as their rank, but they were commonly addressed as colonel, not lieutenant colonel. Higher-ranking colonels like Oscar Reed wore a black-embroidered eagle as their rank. The eagle was the bird in the phrase *full-bird colonel*.

The chain of command was like a ladder. Tom was the company commander of the 584th Military Police Company. He was responsible for every aspect of one hundred and twenty soldiers' lives. The next rung higher was the battalion commander, Lieutenant Colonel Stephens, responsible for four MP companies, including Tom's. The next rung higher was Colonel Reed, commander of the 89th MP Brigade, comprised of five battalions located at five different army bases across four different states. Tom had skipped a rung, a very big rung, to speak to Colonel Reed directly.

Officers did not skip the chain of command.

Tom had. "I haven't spoken with Colonel Stephens yet, sir. I wanted you to hear this first."

"So this isn't official business. Or is this something personal that's about to become official business?"

"This weekend…" Tom stood with his gaze straight ahead, finding it easier to focus on the wall than the man seated at the desk. Colonel Reed wasn't just the brigade commander. He was also Oscar Reed, the man who'd lived next door when Tom was just nine years old. As a junior officer in his early twenties, Oscar and two other new lieutenants had combined their housing allowances to afford a big house with a swimming pool, right next door to Tom's father. Dad had been a fighter pilot and a major in the air force at the time, several ranks higher and at least a decade older than Oscar and the guys. He had not been pleased with the new neighbors.

Tom had been thrilled. Oscar had taken pity on the nine-year-old boy who'd shadowed him, desperate for a role model. For a hero. For a man who paid attention to him.

Oscar hadn't been able to change the oil in his car without Tom wriggling under the car, too. For the three years he'd lived next door, Oscar had patiently looked at every frog and spider Tom had caught. When Tom had decided to serve in the military, he hadn't followed his father into the air force. He'd followed Oscar into the army. Hell, Tom was military police because the young Lieutenant Oscar Reed had been an MP.

To be serving now as a company commander in

Colonel Reed's brigade was an honor. And now, Tom had to tell Oscar Reed what a fool he'd been. *Damn it, Helen. Damn you.*

"This weekend…? This weekend *what*?" Colonel Reed stood suddenly, but he lowered his voice. "Son of a biscuit, Tom, tell me you didn't spend the weekend in jail."

"No, sir."

"You didn't break any laws?"

"No, sir."

"Thank God. That would kill your career. Even I couldn't get that off your record." He nodded toward his office door, always open, part of his personal leadership style. "Go close the door, then put your fourth point of contact in a chair, dagnabbit. You're making me nervous."

Tom almost smiled at that. Oscar was the one and only man in the military who never swore. Tom had assumed he didn't swear around him because he'd been a child, but now, coming back into his life as an adult, he realized that Oscar didn't swear around anyone, of any age.

As Tom sat in the chair just to the left of the desk, the colonel slid his laptop off to the side and folded his hands on top of his desk blotter. "Out with it. What happened in Utah this weekend, besides skiing?"

"There was no skiing. The snow wasn't great. I expected better for the first week of December, but it's been too warm. It rained."

Oscar just raised one brow at him. With a pang, Tom realized that was why he raised one brow as a silent question, too.

"I was stuck indoors with the wedding crowd

around the clock. The wedding was Friday night. By Saturday morning, I couldn't stand any more love and romance and couples talking baby talk to each other everywhere I turned. While I was stuck in the hotel lobby bar, I watched not one, but two, men propose in front of the lobby's goddamned Christmas tree." He glanced at the insignia for a colonel on Oscar's camouflage uniform. "Sir."

"Horrifying. What did you do?"

"I left Utah. I drove two hours to Vegas and got married myself."

The colonel was utterly still for one second. "You're joking."

"I wish I was."

"You got married to *whom*?"

An image of Helen was burned into his mind. A woman with cool elegance. A woman with warm energy. A woman who made him laugh, who listened to him, who opened her heart to him and told him all her hopes and dreams. She could giggle like a child. She could speak with wisdom. And she was sexy, the *sexiest*, the single most sensual woman he'd ever known. His dream girl.

"Some woman I met in a casino." Tom closed his eyes; he didn't need to see the colonel's expression. He rubbed his forehead; he didn't want to remember the moment he'd believed there really was such a thing as love at first sight.

"This was a legal marriage? Not some kind of dress-up photo op at the casino? A bartender didn't officiate? You got a license?"

A license, so easy to get, so ridiculously cheap. A ring—he'd dropped a few thousand there, then a thousand more on the best suite in the hotel for their wedding night. Helen had insisted on paying for her own dress.

"Yes, sir, all legal. She wants a divorce. Already." Saying that sentence caused him pain. He should be feeling no pain; his heart was walled shut. *You don't want me? Then I don't want you.*

The colonel shook his head. "There has to be some easier way out of this. It's been less than a day, hasn't it?"

Tom did the math. "I've been married for thirty-four hours, sir. The Happiest Wedding Chapel did its due diligence in making sure we understood this was a legally binding ceremony."

No backsies, Helen had said with a wink, because it was absurd to even imagine they'd want to change their minds.

Colonel Reed kept shaking his head and pulled his laptop closer. "Where did this wedding take place?"

"The Happiest Wedding Chapel. That's the name of the place. You didn't think I was actually using the word *happiest* to describe any of this stupidity, did you?"

The colonel rolled his eyes and chuckled as he hit a few keys. "No, but let's keep this in perspective. You didn't commit a crime. It's not like you're in here confessing that you're a drug addict or something. A divorce is a pain in the rear, that's all. This will become a story you can tell when you're an old man like me, to prove you once had a wild youth."

Wild youth? Tom was twenty-seven, a company commander with one hundred and twenty lives in his keeping. There was nothing either wild or youthful about military responsibilities. Colonel Reed was forty-two, a man in his prime, not old. The colonel was exaggerating, cracking a joke, trying to lighten the moment.

Tom tried to laugh, but thirty-four hours ago, he actually had been the happiest he'd ever been, and it didn't make him happy to come to that realization while the colonel was typing on his laptop.

"Your chapel's got quite the website. There's got to be something about a twenty-four-hour cooling off period or morning-after annulments—"

"No, sir. We have to get a divorce."

"That's a nuisance… Well, looky here. They've got videos. Tell me there's a video of this debacle. I have to see it to believe it."

Ah, hell.

Colonel Reed was clicking his mouse with a little too much glee. "Look at this. You can watch anyone's wedding. It says they keep it available for ten days— what a scam. They keep the video up so your friends and family can use the convenient links to send gifts to the bride and groom. Man, what an industry this is. They married someone every half hour this weekend. Every half hour! Was Elvis there? Did your bride wear showgirl sequins? Strategically placed feathers?"

"Oscar." *Shut up.*

Tom hadn't called the man by his first name in the three months he'd been under his command. Oscar had been his friend for almost twenty years, the big brother he'd never had. Colonel Reed was his commander.

It didn't faze the colonel. He just waved a hand Tom's way. "Okay, okay. Let me see this for myself."

The laptop started playing familiar music, a contemporary song he and Helen both loved—of course. They'd been in sync about everything.

Tom cleared his throat, but he didn't speak. He had nothing to say.

"Here comes the bride," Colonel Reed said, shaking his head and laughing, like he couldn't believe this was real.

It was real.

"Oh." The colonel blinked at his screen. He glanced at Tom. "She's a knockout. Not in a stripper-pole-dancer kind of way."

Tom glared at him. What was he supposed to say? Thank you?

Colonel Reed was concentrating on the video, serious now. "Look at you. Look at you both."

"No, thank you."

"It's like— It's not what I was expecting. It's like a real wedding. You had your blue mess uniform with you? Oh, right. From the Utah wedding. She's very beautiful. Classy looking."

The colonel finally fell silent, only that made things worse, because now Tom could hear Helen's voice on the laptop's weak speaker. She made him promises she'd had no intention of keeping.

She can't remember. That wasn't intentional.

She'd refused to stay and even try to remember. She'd cut and run.

Colonel Reed casually angled the screen so Tom could see it, the last thing he wanted to see. There was Helen, so beautiful in her white dress.

Stone. I'm made of stone.

The officiant spoke. "I now pronounce you man and wife. You may kiss the bride." A handful of red rose petals were gently sprinkled over their heads, a blessing.

Tom looked away. He wasn't going to watch this, but then there were the sounds of a scuffle on screen, and he looked back. The chapel doors had burst open, and young, rowdy men had come charging down the aisle. They'd been looking for a cell phone they'd left behind—they'd been part of the wedding a half hour before Tom's. But they'd been drunk and loud and Tom had instantly pulled Helen behind himself to protect her. She was an army officer, he knew that, and she was in great shape physically, he knew that intimately, but she'd been wearing a floor-length, slim-fitting dress, not clothing for self-defense. And she'd been his bride.

Nobody would hurt his bride.

The video ended.

"I'm sorry." Colonel Reed somberly closed his laptop and stood, causing Tom to come to his feet, as well. Captains didn't stay seated when colonels stood, even colonels who'd said *Call me Oscar* to a kid in elementary school.

"Sorry for what, sir?"

"Tom." He sighed as if he'd said much more and checked his watch. "It's almost noon. Let me take you to lunch somewhere off post. We'll talk."

There were two knocks on the office door, quick, cursory. The door opened before Colonel Reed could say *enter*. A sergeant abruptly stopped short with the doorknob in his hand. "Excuse me, sir. I thought you had left for lunch. I'm sorry. I was just coming in to see if you'd left the papers on your desk for the incoming officer. I didn't know you were—"

"Understood. Has she arrived yet?"

"Yes, sir. She's right here."

"Send her in." The colonel glanced at Tom. "Stand by. This won't take a moment."

Tom walked away from the desk to stand near two wingback chairs in a corner, which meant he didn't see the person who rapped on the frame of the open door, two firm knocks.

But he heard a woman speak. "Good morning, sir."

Tom turned around, and his bride walked in the door.

Helen strode into her new brigade commander's office and stood at attention in front of his desk.

Thank God for military courtesies. No matter how exhausted she was, she could function in this setting. She knew what to wear—her camouflage ACUs, or Army Combat Uniform—and she knew the brigade commander would be wearing exactly the same thing. Only their ranks and the sewn-on last names over their right pockets were different. She knew how to stand—heels together, arms straight at her sides, hands in loose fists, thumbs pointing downward. She knew to keep her gaze straight ahead, her chin level.

And, despite an eighteen-hour drive that had extended to twenty hours because of a lengthy detour around a massive wreck in Albuquerque, despite the gritty feeling of her eyeballs and the way her brain was clamoring for sleep, she knew what to say: "Good morning, sir. Captain Helen Pallas, reporting as ordered."

She'd made it just before noon. Thank goodness. If only Tom Cross could see her now, standing at attention in uniform at the desk of the 89th MP Brigade commander and provost marshal of Fort Hood, then Tom would understand why she'd had to leave their little Vegas fantasy so quickly. Why she'd had to leave *alone*.

The brigade commander didn't return her greeting. She waited.

The colonel didn't say anything. He did not tell her to have a seat or even to stand *at ease*.

Great. He was going to be one of those jerks who liked to toy with those in their command, putting them through all kinds of nonsensical tests.

Fine. She could stand here all day in silence.

With a soft curse that sounded suspiciously like "cheese and crackers," the colonel dropped the papers he held and stabbed the space bar on his laptop. He looked at the screen. He looked at her. "Captain Pallas…"

What? At ease? Have a seat? Welcome to Fort Hood? What?

He looked to a corner of the room behind her. "Captain Pallas, I believe your husband is here."

What? Good God, what was her ex doing now? She felt her blood run cold. There was no limit to the lows to which Russell Gannon would stoop. He was leaving Seattle to be stationed at Fort Hood, too, of course— their joint domicile had been set before they'd gotten their divorce—but he shouldn't be moving for a couple of weeks yet, and he had no earthly reason to be at the 89th MP Brigade headquarters in any case. He was a chemical corps officer, not military police. The only reason he could be here was to stir up trouble for her.

When she'd been a company commander, spouses

and ex-spouses of the soldiers in her command had come to see her, often to demand money, reporting a failure to pay child support or alimony. Twice, civilian women had come to Helen's office, accusing their enlisted husbands of adultery, demanding courts-martial for what was, in the military, a legal offense. Once, a man had come to demand that she, the company commander, order his enlisted wife to move back home from a lover's house. The emotional drama was detrimental to what the military called *good order and discipline*, so commanders did have to deal with their soldiers' relationship problems. She'd handled each case, using her legal authority and her common sense. Never had Helen expected to be the one in trouble, rather than the one adjudicating the situation.

All this went through her mind in a flash: *Good God, what is Russell doing now?*

But then the colonel spoke toward someone behind her and said, "Tom, you left a key fact out of your story."

Tom?

"Helen."

That voice. Oh, that voice—it woke up parts of her tired brain, her tired body—but the word *husband* hadn't made her think of Tom for even a second. Russell was her husband, *had been* her husband, and he was awful. More awful than she would have believed if she hadn't lived it. But Tom? Tom was barely her husband, if he was her husband at all. She hadn't had any time to verify that his story was true and a marriage license existed.

Thank God, again, for military training. Helen kept her chin up as she turned around. There he was, not her ex-husband, but Tom Cross, standing there in the same uniform she wore.

Damn, he looked good. *I slept with that.*

He was in the army—had she known that? He wore the same captain's bars as she did. She tried to remember.

Nothing. There was no specific memory, but somehow, she had known he was in the service. Maybe it was because his haircut looked military even in the civilian world of Las Vegas. It wasn't something she'd consciously thought about at the hotel, because every man in her world had a military haircut, but it must have registered subconsciously.

Or maybe it was the way he'd carried himself with a confident military bearing, even when he'd been wearing no more than a towel. As she looked at him in his uniform, the vision of him gorgeously, gloriously nude was the one thing that was easy to remember. She knew exactly what his chest looked like under that camouflage. She knew exactly how his skin tasted.

She needed to stop remembering that. Captains didn't get flushed in their colonels' offices.

It was incredible to be standing in the same office as Tom. He'd known she had to report in by noon at Fort Hood, and he'd gone to the trouble of finding out where and in which unit she'd be. He'd come to find her.

Something—hope? No. Vanity, perhaps. Something made her heart beat hard, so hard it hurt. Tom Cross must have strong feelings for her. He wasn't letting her slip away so easily.

Oh, Tom. I'm so sorry, but I don't know you.

But wait—

Tom. The commander, Colonel Reed, had called him *Tom.* He'd said Tom had already told him their *story.* With a jolt, Helen realized Tom had tracked her down, but only so he could beat her here and talk to her brigade commander before she could. About what?

Relationship drama, detrimental to good order and discipline. There was nothing else to talk about. This was no grand romantic gesture; this was professional sabotage.

"I take it this is a surprise for all three of us." Colonel Reed sat behind his desk and made a magnanimous, sweeping gesture with his hand. "Go on. You two catch up."

Helen walked over to the wingback chairs and, for the sake of privacy, stood close to Tom.

He faced her as a soldier faced inspection. His face had no expression at all. Not aggression, not curiosity. No welcome. Certainly, no warmth.

She kept her voice pitched low, although the commander could probably still hear everything. "Are you stationed at Fort Hood?"

"Yes." He bit the word out. So much for being a lover who hadn't wanted to let her go. *Never expect anything else, ever.*

"Why did you track me down like this? I told you I'd take care of the legalities. Did you think I wouldn't keep my word?"

He narrowed his gaze at that. "Did you change your mind?"

"Of course not," she hissed. "I promised you I'd get the divorce under way, and I will, but I just got on post half an hour ago. I haven't had a chance to even type 'how to get a Las Vegas divorce' into a search bar yet. Cut me some slack. I've been driving for twenty hours. You knew I would be."

He looked at her for the longest time, an eternal moment. "I'm glad you made it here in one piece. You look exhausted."

"Thank you so much." *I feel worse.* "So then, why are you standing in my brigade commander's office?"

"Because," he said, as he turned just an inch, so she could see the unit patch on his shoulder, "he's my brigade commander, too."

She rocked back on her heels as all her expectations exploded in front of her. She'd planned to make her first impression here without anyone knowing that she had a stupid, quickie, Vegas marriage to unravel. Nobody would need to know she'd had such a lapse in judgment. She wouldn't lose their respect before she'd had a chance to earn it.

At Lewis-McChord, when she'd had to change the name tags on her uniforms from Gannon back to Pallas, the reactions had all been negative. Either she'd been pitied as a doormat who'd let her man walk all over her, or she'd been labeled a bitch who'd driven her man away. She'd been told that she should have tried harder if she took her marriage seriously. She'd been told that she shouldn't have ever tried to be a wife in the first place, not if she was serious about her career.

She'd been so relieved to leave Seattle.

Fort Hood would be a fresh start. She would arrive at the 89th MP Brigade with her maiden name sewn permanently on her uniforms, and her failed marriage to Russell Gannon would be something that no one here would have heard about. For the last twenty hours, she'd clung to the fact that no one at Fort Hood would hear about her momentary insanity in Vegas, either. She and Tom would quietly get a divorce, a mere filing of paperwork to countermand the chapel's paperwork, and what happened in Vegas would stay in Vegas.

Tom had ruined everything.

She put a hand on the back of the chair to steady herself and concentrated on the grain of the leather upholstery. "Who else have you told?"

"No one."

"Can we keep it that way?"

He didn't answer her.

She looked up into his face, that handsome face with those bluer-than-blue eyes, and some part of her instinctively felt safe with him. It was that Pavlovian response again: he was trustworthy.

But he was not. He'd talked to her commander without talking to her first. He'd betrayed her.

Tears stung her eyes. She was too damned tired, just physically worn out, to deal with this now. Behind her, Colonel Reed had started typing on his laptop, but she was acutely aware that he must be watching this surprise meeting. She looked into Tom's eyes and silently mouthed one word: *Please?*

He dropped his gaze, and she realized he was looking at her left hand as she clutched the back of the chair. Her knuckles were white with the effort it was taking to keep herself together.

"If you want this to be a secret, why are you wearing your ring?"

She snatched her hand off the chair. She'd given up trying to twist that ring off about eight hundred miles ago. She'd forgotten she was wearing it at the moment, frankly—it didn't feel strange or unusual. She could only assume that was because she'd had another band on that same finger for two years.

"I didn't want to lose it. You can have it." She twisted it once more, but it was still stuck. She held her hand out. "It won't come off. You try."

He took her fingers in his hand and looked at the band, a thin circlet of tiny diamond chips that managed to be fancy and yet simple at the same time, a nearly flat band that had no setting sticking up that might get caught on olive drab equipment, a good choice for a woman who wore a uniform every day. He looked from the ring to her. "No."

"No?"

He let go of her hand. "I put that ring on your finger. I'm not going to take it off. You want it off, you take it off yourself. I never will."

Her lips parted in surprise, but she didn't make a sound. Nothing made a sound—not her, not Tom, not even the brigade commander, who was no longer typing. In the silence, Helen's heart beat as if the man before her had said something romantic, but the hard look on his face had nothing of love in it. It was a challenge. He was going to make her be the bad guy.

The brigade commander cleared his throat. "Well, now that you've had a chance to say hello, sit down, both of you."

Tom took the seat to the left of the desk. Helen took the one to the right. They sat as stiffly as if they were still standing at attention. Neither of them spoke.

The colonel sat back and looked between them. "I watched your wedding video online."

There was an online video? Helen gave up and let

her shoulders droop. This was a frigging nightmare. Professionally, personally…nightmare, nightmare.

"I want to know what happened between that ceremony and now? Why are you two so…at odds?"

Helen looked at Tom, who looked at her. *He doesn't know what to say, either.*

"Let me try this again. Captain Cross tells me you want a divorce. Is that true, Captain Pallas?" The colonel's tone of voice demanded an answer.

Helen took a slow breath. It was time to salvage what she could from this disastrous introduction to her superior officer. "We're not at odds, sir. We are in agreement that we'll get a divorce as soon as possible."

"Why?"

"We met and married the same day, sir. It was… illogical to get married. We're strangers."

"You didn't look like strangers at the altar," he replied.

Sleep deprivation was making her delirious, because the colonel sounded almost sad. Kindly, paternal, sad.

Tom interrupted. "She doesn't remember the ceremony, sir. She doesn't remember anything. She— we—must have celebrated too hard."

She felt flushed from different emotions. Embarrassment, anger—Tom made her sound like a blackout drunk.

I know better. She didn't know why she couldn't remember much about Vegas, but she'd never been a heavy drinker. She resented being painted as one now, here, in front of her new commander.

"That's not true, sir. I remember some things." She stated it as the truth that it was—but there was no way she could look at Tom, because he knew exactly what one thing she remembered.

Roses are always going to remind me of sex with you.

She kept her expression neutral. "But what I remember is not enough to base a marriage on, sir."

Tom's expression wasn't quite neutral. She could see that he was clenching his jaw, probably biting back a comment about her memories that the colonel shouldn't hear.

The colonel let them stew in silence for a good, long moment. "In the end, only the two of you can decide that."

"Yes, sir," Helen answered dutifully. She already knew the truth, though. She'd learned it the hard way in Seattle with another man. She wasn't very good at being a wife. She didn't care to try again and prove that twice.

"Now that we've got the initial shock over with, let's try this again. Good morning, Captain Pallas. Welcome to Fort Hood."

"Thank you, sir."

"You're authorized five business days to complete your move to Fort Hood. You know the drill. Medical records, parking passes, physical fitness test, arranging delivery of your household goods."

"Yes, sir."

"Tomorrow will be day one. Today, you need to recover. Get some sleep. You've had a big weekend, you've been driving for twenty hours straight—"

Damn it. The colonel had heard every word she and Tom had exchanged in the corner.

"—and you've apparently had quite the surprise just now. Regroup. Recover. Sleep. Got it?"

"Yes, sir."

"Tom, there's been a change in our lunch plans, obviously. Escort your wife to your house instead."

"Sir?" Tom sounded as if he wasn't sure he'd heard that incorrectly.

Helen rushed to clear up the colonel's misunderstanding. "I'm going to check into the BOQ, sir. Or VOQ." An apartment- or hotel-style building on every post served as the BOQ, or Bachelor Officer Quarters, a place where single officers could live either permanently or for a few weeks while house-hunting. A big post like Hood might have a separate VOQ, Visiting Officer Quarters.

Colonel Reed corrected her. "There is no BOQ on post, Captain Pallas. It's been privatized. It's now a Holiday Inn."

That sounded good to her.

Colonel Reed lined through an item on her paperwork and initialed it. "But you are no longer authorized a stay there. You are not a single soldier."

"I really am, sir. Vegas was a mistake. We're planning on a divorce."

"You are not in any physical danger from your spouse, are you?"

"No, sir, of course not."

"Then you will reside in the housing the army has provided. Tom already lives in a single-family home designated for a captain. Or captains."

She looked at Tom in alarm. He took over the argument. "Colonel Reed, I need to point out that this would be a waste of time and energy. Once we're divorced, she would have to move all her household goods again."

The colonel raised one brow. "Do either of you know how long a divorce takes?"

She only knew the law in Seattle, Washington, where she'd married Russell. She wasn't going to tell the colonel she'd already been divorced once. She'd seem deranged, getting married again so quickly in Las Vegas, Nevada.

"No, sir," Helen said. "I haven't had time to look up Nevada's laws."

"Nevada has nothing to do with it," the colonel said. "That's where you got married. You must file for divorce in the state you live, and that is now Texas."

Helen had a sinking feeling she wasn't going to like Texas's law.

"One of you has to have lived in Texas for six months before you can begin the legal process—and yes, that is true of active duty military personnel, too."

"Six months?" That sinking feeling plunged to rock bottom. Seattle had only required ninety days. "In that case, sir, I definitely need to have my own housing."

"Your spouse has already secured your quarters."

"I can't impose on Captain Cross for half a year." She glanced at Tom. He looked as incredulous as she felt. It was his house, after all, that he was now being forced to share. She spoke to him apologetically. "I'll pay for my own place off post."

The colonel didn't miss a beat. "I require you to live on post."

That was outrageous. Technically, yes, a commander could require his key personnel to live on post, but it was so rarely done. Besides, an assistant brigade S-3 was an important job, but no more rare or vital than any other staff position.

As if they were a tag team, Tom jumped in again. "Sir, you can't do this."

"Is that so, Tom? A service member reports to my unit already married to another service member. That service member—you, Tom—already resides in adequate and appropriate post housing commensurate with her rank. No married couple gets two separate houses from the US Army. Your wife will live with you for as long as you have a wife."

Beside her, Tom sucked in a quick breath, a hiss in reverse. They had to get divorced. It was the only way around this.

"Have you already lived in Texas for six months?" she asked Tom. He'd said if she wanted a divorce, she'd have to file, but surely he would rather do the filing than have a roommate forced upon him.

"I've been stationed here for three months."

"So, with you as the petitioner, we have three to go, not six. I'll be the respondent." She ignored the way Tom narrowed his eyes in displeasure at her assumption that he would file, and she turned to Colonel Reed. "Only twelve weeks, sir. I am basing my request for my own housing on practicality. We anticipate being legally single again in a matter of weeks."

"Denied. I'm not required to provide separate houses for a married couple who merely *anticipate* that they will file for a divorce at some point in the future."

"But, sir—"

"Let me tell you what else I'm not required to do. I'm not required to facilitate that divorce. You've had command, Captain Pallas. You have command now,

Captain Cross. You both know that what commanders are required to facilitate are the health, welfare and morale of those under their command. Roger?"

She and Tom exchanged a glance before they nodded.

"You both appear to think that living together in the housing that the military has provided will be stressful. Therefore, for the sake of your health, welfare and morale, I am ordering you to attend counseling. Marriage counseling."

Helen was stunned into silence.

Tom spoke for her. "You can't do that, sir."

"I must do that. What kind of commander would I be to leave you two in distress? You will attend weekly marriage counseling sessions. Until you actually go to a courthouse and file for divorce, you are married."

"Marriage counseling?" Helen repeated. Her voice sounded faint. How appropriate. She felt faint.

"Don't worry. The behavioral health office will send me a report, but it won't include any specifics. They'll verify your attendance, and they will confirm that you are both capable of performing your military duties while undergoing therapy. I won't get any juicy details."

"Juicy details." Tom sounded furious, not faint in the least. "I cannot believe you're even—"

"Enough." The colonel abruptly stood and smacked both hands on his desk, leaning toward them to close the distance. He was furious, in full drill instructor mode. "On your feet."

She and Tom stood without hesitation.

"Let's go through this one last time, since neither

one of you bright young officers seems to be able to comprehend one basic fact. *Are you married?*"

"Yes, sir," she and Tom answered in unison.

The colonel handed Helen her paperwork. "End of discussion. Captain Cross, give your wife a key to your house, and notify me of the date of your first counseling appointment. It needs to be in one week or less. You are both dismissed."

An order was an order. Side by side, like obedient new recruits, Helen and Tom executed identical about-faces and headed for the door.

"One more thing," the colonel called after them, sounding suddenly, jarringly jovial. "Congratulations."

Chapter Four

Tom checked his rearview mirror.

His wife was trailing him in her sturdy Volvo, keeping a safe distance.

Just what every groom hopes for on his honeymoon: a bride who keeps a safe distance.

They passed a patrol car coming from the other direction. The MP flashed his red and blue lights for just a second, recognizing his company commander's personal vehicle.

Tom raised a hand in casual acknowledgment. He wished he were still a young lieutenant pulling duty, riding around in a patrol car, counting the hours until he could go blow off some steam. He wished he were pretty much anywhere, doing anything besides leading Helen Pallas to his house. It felt more like he was dragging her there. Under orders.

This wasn't how it was supposed to be.

"I live on post. It's not mandatory for company commanders to live on post, but it's highly encouraged. You know how 'highly encouraged' works. Housing is currently underutilized at Fort Hood, so bachelor officers can be assigned a single-family home. I've got two bedrooms and one bath with a garage. Plain white walls. Same as every house on the street. All my neighbors are bachelors, too. The army filed us neatly on one block."

Helen laughed at his description. *"That's so military. All of it."*

They were waiting their turn outside the tiny wedding chapel. In another half hour, this beautiful woman would become his wife. The rest of his life would be full of making memories with her, but he wanted this one to always be crystal clear, the way she looked now, in her wedding gown.

He'd thought the dress looked too plain on the store's hanger, a floor-length column of white, unadorned by a single sequin or scrap of lace. But when Helen wore it, the soft material skimmed over her figure, dipping where it should dip, curving where she curved. She'd come out of the store's dressing room absolutely beaming, absolutely beautiful, when she'd tried it on.

"This one," she'd said.

"That one," he'd agreed.

She was radiant still, luminous even after midnight in this little chapel courtyard. The desert breeze blew her hair forward, so it brushed her cheeks and lips. Her hair was all one length, just short enough that it would brush the collar of her uniform, if she were *wearing one. By regulation, that meant it was just short enough that she would not have to wear her hair pulled back tightly in a bun when she was in uniform. He thought that was smart of her; those tight buns full of pins had to get uncomfortable. He liked her hairstyle for a less practical reason. It was sensual. Her hair swished when she moved, touchable, soft— so feminine compared to his military cut. Smart and sensual, that was his bride. The best of both worlds. The best of everything.*

She turned her face into the breeze, letting it blow her hair back into place. "If you're trying to scare me off by telling me you live on post, it isn't working. I've been in the army two years longer than you have. I've seen my share of outdated kitchens."

"It's got a decently modern kitchen, actually. You've been in the service three years longer, by the way. I goofed off for a year after college. You like to mention that you're older than I am, don't you? I think you like the idea that you're robbing the cradle by marrying me."

She fussed with the bow tie of his blue mess uniform. He'd worn the army's most formal uniform with its gold-braid epaulettes to his friend's wedding yesterday. He was getting married in it today.

Helen smoothed her palm up the satin of his lapel and tilted her face up to his. He set his hands on her waist, the white material of her dress smooth against his palms. Her skin was smoother, he knew from their afternoon by the resort pool. Arousal simmered between them. This was going to be the wedding night of all wedding nights.

"I'm not thinking of cradle-robbing when I look at

you. When I look up at you. You're taller than I am. Bigger. Stronger. Can I tell you a secret? One I'd have to deny if you ever repeated it? I spend my whole life being strong enough and tough enough to be a soldier, but deep down, I have a secret fantasy that, at least for a little while, I'd like to be fragile. Or little. Delicate? I don't know the right word."

He smiled at her because she was smiling as she spoke, but he sensed there was a real yearning in there somewhere. It couldn't be easy to be a woman in a man's world.

Her smile was fading as she spoke. "The truth is, you look terribly masculine in uniform. Just so strong and capable. And the truth is, my first instinct is that I must rise to the challenge. I have to be as good at being an officer as you are. As good as every other officer in the whole army. I realize you'd win every push-up challenge, but I still have to be able to do enough push-ups for the job. I have to be really good at all the other things—have endurance and make good decisions under stress. That's the reality. But..."

She'd been looking at his chest, even running her fingertips lightly over the rows of ribbons, but now she looked up at him through her lashes, pressing her body closer to his in a clearly sensual way. He breathed in deeply, tightened his hold on her waist.

"...that's not the fantasy. This uniform, all these medals that prove what a badass you've been in the army...you're incredibly appealing to me. The fantasy is that I don't have to be like you at all. You make me wish I was a delicate little Snow White, who had a prince just scoop her into his arms like she was as light as a feather, tra-la, tra-la. She didn't have to do

a thing as her prince carried her away, except laugh and kick her delicate feet and wave at the woodland creatures. Just for a little while, it would be so nice..."

Once again, her smile faded into something more earnest. "I meant everything we talked about, though. I would never expect you to shoulder every burden while I just sat around, looking pretty. We'll be a team, you and me against the world. I'm only talking about a fantasy. It's just that when you look so damned... macho...it brings out this side of me that... I don't know. I probably shouldn't wish that I was fragile, even for a night, not when I can't be like that in real life. But...well, anyway."

Tom scooped her up like a groom carrying his bride over the threshold. She might not think her tall and toned body was as light as a feather, but to him, she was. He could bench-press triple her weight. He did bench-press triple her weight, several days a week. "Your fantasies are really too easy."

It took her a moment to relax, a moment before she realized he wasn't straining to hold her. Her nervous laugh subsided, and she laid her head on his shoulder, nuzzling into the space between the side of his neck and the gold-braided epaulettes. "Maybe you think it's easy because you aren't a fantasy. You really are this big, strong man in uniform. But I'm not really a delicate princess."

"I know that. There's no such thing as a fragile little soldier in real life, but you can be my light-as-a-feather girl anytime you want. It'll be our secret."

"You can carry me around inside our house on post."

"Nobody will see."

"In that case, you might as well carry me around naked."

They were laughing again. Always. The strains of a trumpet voluntary drifted from the chapel into their courtyard.

"I have another confession," she said.

"Can't wait."

"I know you're trying to set my expectations pretty low for on-post housing, but do you have any idea how lovely it will be to arrive on a post for the first time in my life without needing to find a place to live?" She fingered his black bow tie. "It feeds right into that helpless princess fantasy. I won't have to make any decisions. I won't have to decide whether to buy or rent. I won't have to negotiate a contract and be on guard against being taken advantage of. I won't even have to get the electricity and water turned on. My big, strong man has already taken care of all that."

Tom heard what she didn't say. She'd done all the work at her last post. At every post, of course, while she'd been single, but at her last post, she'd had a husband who should've helped. He hadn't.

Tom kissed her hair. "Did you have a hard time finding a place to live near Seattle?"

She picked up her head to look at him. "Am I that easy to read? It was hard. Mostly because my ex had very picky requirements he expected me to find. I want you to know that I will never be that picky about houses with you."

"Likewise. We'll just assume that's covered in the vows. I think 'for better or worse' makes a good catch-all. If the housing around our next post sucks, we won't make it harder than it has to be."

"*I love the way you interpret those vows. I'm so happy I'm going to marry you.*"

He kissed her. It was all he could do, because he didn't have the words to tell her how he felt. It was almost disorienting to love someone so wholeheartedly. It was a new kind of freedom, to just let go and be in love.

He set her down gently, so she stood on the first step of the chapel. "*Tell me about the house in Seattle. Do you still own it?*"

"*No. Russell demanded it be sold as part of the divorce. It sold quickly, thankfully. One less thing to keep me entangled with him.*"

When the breeze blew her hair across her cheek, Tom smoothed it back and kept his hand there, cupping her head. "*Were you sad to sell it? That's a raw deal, being forced to sell a house you'd worked so hard to find.*"

"*It was never the perfect house, even though I'd managed to check most of the boxes on Russell's list. It was just an adequate house, according to him. Since he was going to have a spectacular life without me around, he didn't want the adequate house. He so very generously decided the adequate couch and the adequate kitchen table could go with me. He'll have no place for them in his spectacular new life.*"

She rolled her eyes in mild disgust, but she also pressed her cheek into his hand. She had no tender feelings toward her ex. Of that, Tom was certain. But the divorce hadn't been free of pain.

"*The movers are on their way. I'm afraid a very adequate set of furniture will be arriving on your doorstep shortly after I do.*"

"Yours will be joining an adequate set of my own furniture in my own adequate quarters. But if we decide we don't like it, we're going to go buy what we like. We'll live where we want to. We're done letting our lives be adequate. It might have been okay for me. It might have been okay for you. But for us? The two of us, together? We'll never settle for adequate again."

Tom pulled into his driveway and waited for Helen to catch up. He looked at his house, a cookie-cutter government house, but it had a decent number of windows, a bit of a front porch. Two bedrooms.

Helen pulled in. He got out of his car as she got out of hers.

"Nice house," she said.

"I'd describe it as *adequate*."

She nodded. "Adequate for the task at hand. Since it has two bedrooms, I'll be able to stay out of your way as much as possible."

We'll never settle for adequate again.

But she didn't remember that.

Adequate, it would be.

The first time Helen woke up, it was pitch black.

She didn't know where she was for a moment, but then it all came crashing in. The twenty-hour drive, the brigade commander roaring *Are you married?* She remembered that she was in Tom Cross's house, ordered to live with a man who might legally be her husband but who was practically a stranger. An incredibly sexy stranger.

Was a man a stranger if you'd had sex with him? Once? Well, once that she could remember clearly.

She rolled onto her back and blinked at the night.

The last time she'd woken up, she'd been in a gold bed filled with roses. She'd wandered into the living room. Tom Cross had walked in, told her she was beautiful, that he was afraid he'd dreamed her and then he'd kissed her. The man kissed like a dream. He kissed…generously. Asking with soft lips if she'd like it harder. Asking with a gentle tongue if she'd like the kiss to deepen.

"I sure answered that," she whispered in the dark. She'd practically dragged him down to the couch with her. She might have been the one underneath, but she'd had her way with him. He'd been as generous with his body as he'd been with his mouth, reading her reactions to every move, giving her more of anything that made her arch her back or tighten her thighs around him.

For those moments, she'd felt like she knew what she wanted and with whom she wanted it. But then, as their breathing had slowed and their heartbeats had returned to normal, she'd felt so very disoriented. Why wasn't she on her way to an army base? Why was there a wedding band on her hand?

She'd looked at Tom's face and realized she didn't know anything about him, except he had a generous mouth and an indulgent body. But he'd expected her to know him. He'd said things she had no knowledge of. He'd asked questions she didn't know the answers to.

Then he'd been hurt.

Then he'd turned cold.

She was no good at this. She was a terrible partner, never considerate enough of the other person's feelings. Russell had been hurt that she was always misconstruing the things he said. *I didn't say I had the right to decide whether your hair should be short or long; I just asked you whose opinion matters more to you than your husband's.* Russell had gotten tired of waiting for her to grow into her role as his wife. He'd turned cold, too. The divorce had been his idea.

She'd been sincere in the hotel suite when she'd told Tom he was fortunate that she was getting out of his life immediately. She was not cut out for marriage. But then Tom had had the nerve to order her to stay, to eat, to let him drive her car. When he'd physically restrained her with a hand on her arm...

She must have been insane to agree to marry that man. She didn't want to be married again to anyone, let alone to a man who felt he owned her.

She sat up and checked the time on the fitness band on her wrist. It was past one in the morning, but she'd been sleeping for more than ten hours. The second bedroom didn't have a bed, but the futon sofa had looked like heaven when she'd adjusted it to lay flat. The moment Tom had silently grabbed a few pieces of workout gear from his spare bedroom and left her alone, she'd untied her combat boots, yanked them off and fallen onto the flat mattress, out like a light at three in the afternoon.

Tom's spare bedroom. Tom Cross. Captain Tom Cross, legally my husband.

It was incomprehensible that she was truly the wife of another army officer and stuck living with him for at least three months. The thought of it made her jaw clench, her fists clench. Reality hurt.

She could do nothing about it.

Focus on what you can change.

Well, she was thirsty and she was starving. She could at least fix that.

She ventured out of her bedroom. The ties at the ankles of her ACU pants tickled her bare feet. The house was small. The galley kitchen was walled off from the living room. The two bedrooms and one bathroom shared the same short hallway. Tom's bedroom was dark, the door open. She tiptoed to it, feeling like she was conducting a military op in her camouflage trousers and her brown T-shirt, and closed the door with a silent, steady turn of the knob. She didn't want to wake him with any kitchen noises.

The tile of the kitchen floor was cold on the soles of her feet. Her eyes were already adjusted to the dark, so the glow of the clock on the microwave oven was enough for her to see everything in the small kitchen. She assumed they'd live like college roommates for the next three months, keeping their food on separate shelves, but tonight, his was the only food available. To get her own food, she'd have to get completely dressed, get in her car and drive off post to find a twenty-four-hour grocery store. Then she'd have to go through security to get back on post.

Not happening. Her Vegas husband was going to have to let her borrow his food. Bread and butter wasn't too much to ask for from a man who'd blabbed about their marriage to the brigade commander. If he hadn't done that, Helen would be sleeping in a Holiday Inn right now, not on a futon. She popped two slices of bread in the toaster and took a giant tub of margarine out of the fridge.

The ring on her left hand reflected the refrigerator light.

She shut the door, but she couldn't take her eyes off that ring. Genuine diamonds were like magnets for light. She'd lost her night vision in the bright light of the fridge, so now, in the dark, the only thing she could see was the way the diamonds on her finger refracted and reflected the glowing blue numbers on the microwave.

She needed to take this ring off before morning. It would cause everyone to ask questions about her husband. Those were questions she'd rather not answer, considering she would have no husband in twelve weeks. She'd looked it up on her phone's calendar. This was the first week of December. Tom could file for divorce the week after Valentine's Day. She couldn't file until the first week of June. There was no way they'd stay married that long. No possible way.

Helen set the margarine down, all three pounds of it, then gave the ring another twist. Another tug.

She walked over to the sink and turned the water on cold. The cold would make her finger as small as possible, right? But it would also make the metal contract, hypothetically. She turned the faucet to warm and tugged and tugged.

No good.

She shut the water off. The toast popped up, smelling heavenly. She opened a few drawers and found a knife for the margarine. Inspiration struck: margarine was slippery. She took off the tub's lid, scraped a good teaspoon's worth onto the knife, then buttered her finger. *Well, that killed the sparkle of the diamonds.* Silly to miss that sparkle. Rushing now, not wanting her toast to grow cold, she stood over the sink and found that she couldn't get a grip on the ring at all. At the first attempt, both of her hands became a greasy mess.

"What are you doing?"

Helen whirled around, raising one buttered hand in self-defense—which meant offense. She threw a ka-rate chop toward the intruder's windpipe at the same second she realized it was Tom.

He caught her hand, which slipped out of his grip and left his hand slick with margarine. "What the hell?"

"Why did you sneak up on me like that?"

He rubbed the margarine between his fingers. "What *are* you doing?"

She took a pace away from him, adrenaline spiking from the scare. He was still in his camouflage pants and brown ACU T-shirt, like she was. She peeked down the hallway. His bedroom door was still shut. "Where did you come from?"

"Are you eating margarine with your hands?"

"Seriously? Why would I do that?"

"Am I supposed to come up with a serious reason you would do that?"

She huffed impatiently. "Were you in the living room?"

"Is there some reason I shouldn't be in my own living room?"

But in the dim light, she saw him press those tal-ented lips together, trying not to smile.

She frowned. "Are you going to answer my questions or not?"

"Have you asked all the ones you want answered?"

"I—" She squinted at him. "Are you answering my questions with questions?"

The man just grinned in the dark kitchen. He was toying with her. He'd scared her half to death, and now he was playing a game while they stood there in matching brown T-shirts, holding their margarine-greased hands away from their uniforms.

Jeez, she wasn't awake enough for this, but she never backed down from a challenge. Through gritted teeth, she asked, "Do you find yourself amusing?"

He nodded toward the toaster. "Are you hungry?"

"Are you always so observant?"

He smiled openly at that and set his clean hand on the kitchen counter, leaning against the granite. She was amazed the army had actually installed granite in the kitchen.

Tom nodded at the glowing clock on the microwave. "Did you get enough sleep?"

"Does ten hours of uninterrupted sleep sound like enough?"

He tilted his head and looked at her. The blue light of the clock made his blue eyes look an unnatural shade bluer in the dark. Good Lord, the man was gorgeous. Her heart kept beating hard, refusing to calm down now that her scare was over.

"So, are you feeling better now?" he asked.

"Better than what?" But she knew what he was asking. He'd said it at the hotel: *Some coffee, some food, a shower. You'll feel better, and you'll remember, dream girl, you'll remember.*

She couldn't keep looking at him. She looked down at their bare feet. It gave her a sense of déjà vu. When had she seen his bare feet so near to hers before?

I saw his everything less than forty-eight hours ago.

Of course—when she'd had sex with a stranger on a couch in Las Vegas.

She raised her head and shook her hair back, but one strand kind of got stuck on her eyelashes. She automatically raised a hand to brush it back, but stopped herself in the nick of time. Margarine and hair didn't mix. She tried to blow a puff of air at the strand to make it move.

"Since I have a clean hand, can I help?" Tom smoothed the piece of hair out of her eyes, then kept his hand cupping the side of her face, his palm warm over her ear. "Do you remember now? Anything at all?"

He wanted her to. He longed for her to. She could feel the emotion coming from him, his hopes and expectations weighing on her chest until she could no longer breathe from the pressure of it. He was such a beautiful man, holding her so gently, and here she was, helpless to do anything except disappoint another man. Again.

She hated Russell Gannon for being right.

She shook her head. *Nothing.* "Didn't I warn you I wasn't wife material?"

Her words sank in. His hand withdrew. His expression cooled.

She felt like a failure. If she was such a lousy wife, she shouldn't be wearing a ring. Impatiently, she held up her left hand. "Could you help me get this off?" But when she twisted the ring this time, it slipped off so easily, so suddenly, that she dropped it.

She crouched down, looking for it in the dark, not wanting to pat around the floor with her butter hands, feeling like a fool as Tom just stayed where he was while she crouched and twisted to see under the cabinets.

She saw a dull glint, a slightly different shade of darkness, grabbed the ring and stood up. "Can you believe I found it?"

Tom glanced at the clock. "Forty-eight hours. You managed to wear that ring almost exactly forty-eight hours."

Game over. He hadn't phrased his comment as a question. She'd won, but only because he had stopped giving a damn about the game he'd started. Of course. *Come and play with me* had turned into *I don't care.* When would she learn to expect nothing else?

She looked at the clock. "We got married at one thirty-five in the morning?"

But the blue-eyed man who'd teased her with questions was gone; a cold and remote soldier stood in his place. A silent soldier.

Helen returned to the sink to wash the margarine off her hands, stopping up the drain with the sponge first. She didn't want to drop the ring down the drain. Her skin came clean, but the diamond band was still dull. She carefully wiped it on the sponge until it sparkled again. "There. I hope you'll be able to return it. It's only been forty-eight hours."

But he didn't move to take it from her.

She held it out more emphatically. "Take it. It looks expensive. Most jewelry stores have some kind of return policy within a couple of days for engagement sets. You must have a receipt, right?"

She might as well have been air. He didn't move, he didn't respond, he didn't even blink.

The silent treatment. She knew that one so well.

It was infuriating to have a person not even give her the courtesy of a yes or no answer. It made her feel so insignificant—who was she, to think she should even be talking? Russell might have been right that she didn't make a very good wife, but he'd been wrong to freeze her out with silence. She'd had enough of that to last her a lifetime.

"Oh, you're not speaking to me now? Fine." She plunked the ring down on the windowsill over the sink. "Do whatever you want to with the ring. This whole marriage was a mistake, some kind of Vegas craziness that I don't even remember, and I'm just trying to give you this expensive ring back, so at least you aren't out a couple of thousand bucks."

She plucked the two pieces of cold toast out of their chromed slots, stuck the knife in the middle of the giant tub of margarine, picked up the whole tub and started to walk out of the kitchen. Tom stayed exactly where he was. He was blocking her way, just like Russell.

Helen saw red, absolute red. She looked Tom in the eye with all the anger and disgust she felt. Like a drill sergeant, she barked a single word: "Move."

It worked. The silent statue blinked and became a man again. He held his hands up, the fingers on one hand still buttery, and he turned sideways in the narrow kitchen so she could pass.

He even spoke. "I didn't mean to be like— I'm sorry, Helen. I know you hated when Russell did that."

It knocked the wind out of her to hear that man's name on this man's lips. "You—you know who Russell is?"

"Well…" He seemed surprised at her question. "Of

course I do. We couldn't have gotten married if you hadn't gotten divorced."

It was so odd, so very disorienting, to have a stranger know so much about her. She knew nothing about him except how he looked in a towel. He'd known she was in the army, that she was on her way to Fort Hood, that she'd needed to drive through the night. He knew Russell existed. But far more personal than that, Tom knew Russell had penned her in, forcing her to stay in the room and listen to his lectures and tirades, unless she pushed him out of her way to leave. It had always been a toss-up, which one was worse. Listening to all your faults laid bare or being the kind of awful wife who had to physically push her way past her husband to stomp out of the room?

She stared at Tom. It was terrifying, to not know how many of her personal secrets this man might know. She couldn't say anything; she was still trying to get her breath back.

"I'm sorry," Tom said once more. "I'll go wash my hands in the bathroom and go to bed. You stay and eat anything you want here, okay? Two slices of bread can't be enough."

He started to brush her hair back again and she jerked away. She didn't know him. He shouldn't touch her.

He lowered his hand. "That ring is yours, Helen. I gave it to you. Whether you want to wear it or not, it's still yours." He left, walking silently down the dark hall.

She hadn't needed to leave. Tom had left, and not in anger, either.

Helen put the margarine tub down on the counter.

She put the pieces of toast back in the toaster and pressed the lever. Maybe she could get them warm again without burning them all to hell.

Chapter Five

The marriage counselor was a civilian.

Tom assumed that was why she'd come out to the waiting room and cheerfully said, "You must be Mr. and Mrs. Cross," which was completely incorrect. He and Helen were both in their ACUs, so anyone in the military would have easily read their ranks and name tags and addressed them as Captain Cross and Captain Pallas.

It was ironic that the first time he heard the phrase *Mr. and Mrs. Cross*, it was spoken by a marriage counselor. Not a good omen.

In silence, he and Helen followed the counselor down a hall. They'd barely spoken to one another since their Monday night rendezvous in the kitchen. It was amazing how one could share a fairly small house and rarely bump into one another. He worked long days as a company commander. She'd spent the rest of the week around post completing the usual in-processing tasks, or so he assumed. It wasn't like he'd had a chance to ask how her day had been. By the time he came home from work, she'd already made herself dinner—there were clean dishes in the drainboard—and had sequestered herself in his spare bedroom.

Today was Friday. He wondered how they would stay out of each other's way this Saturday and Sunday, with no work to occupy their time.

The counselor, a woman who'd introduced herself as Jennifer, wore slacks and a sweater and a scarf, definitely a government employee rather than a service member. She led the way to an office with upholstered armchairs, soft lighting from a Tiffany-style lamp on a desk, and a little speaker box on the floor of the hallway outside the door. She held the door for them as they walked in, then she tapped the speaker with her toe. Tom heard a white noise like radio static before she shut the door.

"That noise machine is for privacy," she explained. "We don't want anyone walking by to be able to hear what is said through the door."

Juicy details. There weren't any in this marriage. They slept apart, they ate apart, they'd even arrived for this appointment in separate cars from their separate jobs.

All three of them chose chairs and settled in, facing one another in a loose circle. The armchair was the softest thing he'd sat in all week, not firm and cool to the touch like his leather couch at home. It was the complete opposite of a Humvee's canvas seat or a government-issue desk chair at work. Tom sank

into the comfortable cushions and felt acutely uncomfortable.

"So, what brings the two of you in today?"

He exchanged a glance with Helen, but when she
looked away, he did not. He hadn't seen her at all yesterday, not a glimpse, and as he looked at her now, he
realized how much it affected him to just be in the
same room that she was in. *My wife.*

He watched her as she spoke. "We were ordered to
get counseling."

Jennifer looked at her clipboard. "Yes, I see this
visit was mandated by a company...no, a brigade commander. What event prompted the order for you to attend marriage counseling?"

Helen shrugged. "Our marriage did."

"I mean, was there a particular crisis? Typically, a
couple is sent here after a domestic violence incident,
or something else that requires a commander's inter-
vention. For example, one person might lock the other
person out of their house, so the service member has
nowhere to live, and a commander might get involved."

"I guess it's our divorce, then. We told the colonel
that we were getting a divorce, and he ordered us to
come here. We won't meet the residency requirements
to file for a divorce for another twelve weeks, so we're
to come here weekly until then." She said it so calmly,
as though she was describing plans for lunch.

"Are you currently living together?"

"Yes."

"Helen, do you feel safe in your home?"

The implication was offensive, but Tom held his
tongue. He was an MP. Although he rarely patrolled
the garrison as a captain, when he'd been a young lieu-

tenant, he'd been on the scene for too many domestic disturbances. He couldn't imagine hitting a woman in his home, but he knew other men didn't behave the same way. It was a legitimate question.

"If you're asking if Tom is violent, the answer is no." Helen understood the reason for the question as well as he did, since it had turned out she was an MP as well. He'd known in Las Vegas that she was a captain in the army being stationed at Fort Hood. He had not known she was coming to the 89th MP Brigade. The shock of her walking into Oscar Reed's office had been paralyzing.

"Tom, do you feel safe around Helen?"

No. Just looking at her face is breaking down all my defenses. I wanted her. I want her still. I can't make a wall strong enough to keep the pain out. It's killing me.

"Yes," he said. "Fine."

"How long have you two been married?"

"Six days," he said. "We were married Saturday night."

"Ah—oh." Jennifer hadn't expected that answer; he could tell by the way she nearly dropped her pen. "I see."

"Technically, it was Sunday morning," Helen clarified, "but at one-thirty in the morning, so it would have felt like Saturday night."

The only reason she knew that was because he'd told her so when she'd taken off her wedding ring with that damned margarine. The ring was still sitting on the kitchen windowsill, four days later.

Jennifer recovered, smoothing the yellow-lined paper of her legal pad. "And how long were you two a couple before the wedding?"

She'd asked it of Helen, but Helen didn't know. Tom let her squirm for a minute. Six days, and he was already a bitter man. "How long since we first talked, or since we first laid eyes on each other?"

Neither woman answered him.

"We saw each other in the casino earlier in the day, but we first said hello about eleven-thirty in the morning. So, fourteen hours. Then the wedding."

Jennifer was doing her best to school her features into a doctor-like, I've-heard-it-all-before expression, but she wasn't quite pulling it off.

"It was a Vegas thing," Helen said, practically apologizing. "You can see why we need to divorce as quickly as possible. Unfortunately, we have another three months to go before we meet the Texas residency requirements."

"So this was just a spontaneous kind of thing like people do on a whim? Elvis and alcohol, like in the movies?"

"Right," Helen said, grimacing. "It wasn't a serious thing."

Do you take this man to be your lawfully wedded husband? I do.

She'd said *I do*. She'd said it, damn it, after they'd talked for hours about what it meant and how they felt. It hadn't been a joke of a wedding. She'd loved him. She'd believed in *them*, but now she was denying the vows had been real and sincere and warm and healing:

"She doesn't remember."

Both women looked at him in surprise. That had come out sounding more pissed off than he'd intended.

He tried again. "She doesn't remember. We had drinks before the ceremony and drinks to celebrate after, and she woke up in the morning with no memory of the day before. A blackout." Yeah, he was bitter.

"I see. Have you ever experienced a blackout before, Helen?"

"Never. If you're asking if I am an alcoholic or a binge drinker, I am not."

The counselor nodded and turned to him. "And you, Tom? Do you remember?"

"Everything."

He looked at Helen as he said it, looked her in the eyes, and she looked back at him, frightened. The woman he'd held in a chapel courtyard while she'd snuggled into him was *frightened* of him.

With two hands on the overstuffed arms of the chair, he shoved himself to his feet and headed for the door.

"Tom, wait a minute." The counselor stood up and tossed her legal pad on her desk. "I can't imagine how difficult this situation must be for you, so I won't give you any platitudes. But it is my job to help. This is a unique situation. I don't know that we can work to salvage a marriage, because that marriage never really existed."

Wrong. He pulled his patrol cap out of the cargo pocket on his pants, ready to leave.

"Or, to be more accurate, it doesn't exist in one person's mind," Jennifer amended. "What I think you two need to work on is building intimacy with one another."

Intimacy. That got his attention.

Helen looked shocked. "Why would we do *that* when we know we're getting a divorce?"

She'd asked Jennifer, but Tom answered. "Because

you said that you remembered something when we did *that*."

That had been her explanation for why she'd pulled him down onto that couch and made love to him that morning. He'd kissed her again as soon as she'd said it. She'd kissed him back, too, practically going boneless in his arms for a moment, before she'd remembered that she didn't remember who he was.

"I'm not suggesting sexual intimacy," the counselor said smoothly, as if it was standard practice to discuss other people's sex lives. "I think you would benefit as a couple from building emotional intimacy. A personal connection. Not necessarily a romantic one, although that could result from it."

"What other intimacy is there?" Helen sounded as skeptical as Tom felt.

"Think of the word *intimacy* as a technical term, meaning two people who share a closeness that allows them to be in each other's personal space comfortably. You can be intimate in that sense with anyone, such as a parent, a sibling, a best friend. Emotional intimacy does not have to become romance. It doesn't work the other way, however. Romance requires emotional intimacy."

Jennifer sounded like a doctor explaining high cholesterol to a patient as she defined intimacy. "Romantic gestures aren't romantic if emotional intimacy doesn't exist first. Take the traditional gift of a dozen red roses. If I gave a dozen roses to my boss or to my mailman or to anyone else I have not established an emotional intimacy with, the gesture would be so out of place, romance would be the last feeling it inspired.

They'd certainly be uncomfortable. They'd probably feel threatened and wonder what my intentions were."

Roses. Those rose petals had been part of the most erotic lovemaking in his life. He supposed erotic wasn't the same thing as romantic, but the rose petals had been both. Now that he'd laid Helen down in a bed of rose petals, he could never repeat that experience with another woman. Helen had been the pleasure; she'd been the intensity.

He'd requested roses with their wedding breakfast, too. What the counselor was saying made sense: the roses had meant nothing to Helen at breakfast, because she'd lost her memory, and so she'd lost all emotional intimacy with him at that point.

"Since you two are living together, I believe building an emotional intimacy will be beneficial. What do you think?"

Just remembering Helen's smart-aleck salute with the croissant and the way she'd bolted out the door in her wedding gown made his heart want to hide behind every wall he had—and to throw up a few more. There was his answer: building intimacy with Helen again sounded like a terrible idea. Too risky.

"I don't think you can force someone to feel any kind of intimacy with someone else," Helen said.

"Not force someone, I agree," Jennifer said. "But when two people are open to trying certain techniques, there has been some fairly rigorous scientific investigation into building emotional intimacy with a perfect stranger."

A perfect stranger. Helen looked at him, then ducked her chin and looked away. Yeah, he was the perfect stranger in her life. She'd told him so enough times.

"There have been many experiments conducted in that field, and one technique in particular has proven results. Two people sit face-to-face, without any distractions, and ask one another a series of questions. By the time the test subjects get to the last question, the vast majority report that they feel connected to the person who was a randomly assigned stranger at the start of the experiment."

"I've read about this," Helen said, astonishing him. "Aren't there thirty-six questions? I think I read a list of a hundred questions one time. Isn't there an app for this?"

"Twenty questions, sometimes ten. The amount varies from study to study, and it wouldn't surprise me at all if someone had created an app for this. Like many therapists, I use my own set of questions, the ones I've found the most helpful. When we're further along in the process, I may ask you to write your own questions. Our goal is emotional intimacy, not romantic, not sexual."

"Emotional intimacy with a woman who has announced she's divorcing me." Tom remained standing between the chair and the door. This was a terrible idea. He'd leave in a minute.

"Precisely," Jennifer said. "If you are going to begin divorce proceedings in three months, feeling connected to one another in a mutually agreeable, respectful way will make the entire process less stressful. A divorce between two people who don't know what to expect from each other is not likely to go smoothly. Shall we begin?"

It still sounded risky to Tom. He'd be getting attached to a woman who wanted to leave him. But what if she changed her mind? The emotional intimacy might lead to romantic feelings, but that wasn't a guarantee. Tom could fall in love with this new version of Helen like he had with the old, and she could still insist upon a divorce.

Very risky.

When he looked at Helen, she was looking up at him from the soft armchair that was swallowing her, making her look a little vulnerable. A little fragile. Something about the angle of her chin reminded him of the chapel courtyard and her confession. *It would be nice, just once, not to be the one making all the decisions.*

Tom made the decision.

"All right. Let's do this."

Emotional intimacy.

Helen recoiled from the idea of it. Shouldn't they be here to outline their boundaries? To set their limits? To make rules about how they would share his house until the day they could file for divorce and she could move out?

But Tom had said they'd do this, and now they'd moved their chairs so they were facing one another directly, sitting practically knee to knee. A short pile of white index cards sat on a little table beside them. She had no idea what was on them. She had no idea what she was in for.

She didn't want emotional intimacy. She wanted rules.

"Wait," she said. "I thought—I thought we were

going to work out practical matters. We need to decide what to do when my furniture arrives. Should I pay for part of the cable bill when I don't watch TV? I think I should pay for half of the internet connection, because I am using that."

Jennifer looked as if she knew something Helen didn't. Jennifer did not. She had no idea what Helen was thinking and feeling. Helen was thinking that these practical decisions needed to be made. And she was feeling…she was trying not to feel anything at all.

"Those are straightforward decisions that I don't think you need the expertise of a psychologist to make. You seem like two fairly well-adjusted, levelheaded people. You don't need me to do the math of dividing an internet bill in half. Are you ready to begin?"

Helen looked to Tom for help, a strange impulse considering he was the one who had given this a green light. He was watching her as closely as Jennifer had been. What did they think was wrong with her? She just wanted to get something useful out of these mandatory sessions. She realized her arms were crossed over her chest, a defensive posture. She took a breath and uncrossed her arms. "Okay. What are the rules?"

"There are no rules. It's a process. An exploration." The counselor was seated several feet away at her desk. Helen had noticed there were standard fluorescent lights in the office ceiling, but they were off. The Tiffany lamp had a golden glow. Maybe fluorescent lights were bad for mental health. Who knew? Who cared?

I want out of here.

"One of you will draw the top card and read the question out loud. You will both answer. You are talking to each other, so you can discuss the question as long as you like, or you can move on to the next card. Pretend I'm not even here."

As if. Helen snorted in disbelief at that one.

Tom did, too.

Well, look at us, agreeing already.

The counselor got the counseling going. "Read the first question, Helen, when you're ready."

She reached for the first card. Her hand trembled.

Tom nudged her knee with his. "Go ahead. Shoot. I can take it."

"Okay, here goes. 'Would you like to be famous?'" Relief made her smile a bit. That wasn't so bad.

Tom smiled a bit, too, as he sat forward to answer. "No, I don't see any benefit to being famous. I like my career. Being famous would get in the way."

Helen nodded and set the card on the table.

"You're supposed to answer, too." His voice was gentle. He wasn't needling her for forgetting the rules already. He was just prompting her.

"I don't see any benefit to being famous, either. Actually, I take that back. It would be great to get in to see shows and stuff. I'd go to New York and see *Hamilton* and meet Jimmy Fallon and things like that. Then I'd like the fame to disappear. I get the impression that stars have to work pretty hard to maintain it. I don't want to deal with that on a daily basis."

"This isn't so bad," Tom said, as he reached for the next card. Then he read it, and the smile on his face faded. "Would you say your childhood was happier or sadder than average?"

"Wow. That got more personal, fast." *And you don't like it.* And, for some reason, that concerned Helen.

"It's your turn to answer first," Jennifer said from her seat at the desk. So much for forgetting she was there.

Helen watched Tom. He'd already put on a neutral, expressionless expression. She gave her answer to a statue of a soldier. "Before I became an MP, I would have said my childhood was average. Mom, Dad, house in the suburbs, nice public schools. But once I started working garrison as a lieutenant and responded to domestic disturbance calls, I realized my childhood was happier than so many others. My mom fed me three meals a day. My dad never broke my arm to teach me a lesson. It's tragic how many children can't say that."

Tom let the silence last one beat too long. "Same here. Mom fed me. Dad never broke my arm to teach me a lesson."

She kept her gaze steady on his expressionless blue eyes. There was more to his story. He was hiding it. He was hiding everything. This wasn't intimacy.

It doesn't matter. Split the internet bill for twelve weeks.

"Okay, Tom, Helen, our time is up, but this was a good start. We've set a goal, and you've gotten an introduction, at least, to how the process will go. We'll pick up where we left off next week. Thank you for coming in today."

"Oh. Yes." Helen blinked, breaking her connection with his impassive gaze. Everything felt awkward as she tried to get out of the quicksand of the chair. Tom offered her a hand to pull her to her feet when she was already starting to stand, so they bumped into each other, followed by *sorry* and *sorry*. Helen turned to put the table with the cards back against the wall, but Jennifer told her she'd take care of it, so Helen turned toward the door and found Tom waiting there, hand on the knob. He opened it and ushered her out, his hand briefly touching her lower back, such a gentlemanly thing to do while they were both dressed for war.

Get a grip.

As an MP officer, she'd been tested in a thousand scenarios that were more difficult. There was no reason to be flustered now about anything. Tom had retreated behind his military demeanor; so could she. With professionalism firmly in mind, she hesitated in the lobby of the office building. "I'm going to find the restroom."

"Okay." His expression was less stoic now, that stony face softening a bit. "I'll wait here."

"No—I meant you go on ahead. It's not a good idea for us to walk out together. What if someone from the brigade sees us?"

"They'd think we'd both had business in this building?"

She surreptitiously surveyed the nearly empty lobby. Friday evening, there were only a few people still around. This seemed as private a moment as any. "I meant it when I asked you not to tell anyone else that we were married. When I walk into brigade headquarters for my first day of work on Tuesday, how many people are going to ask me about you?"

"Don't worry, Helen." He spoke her name in a low voice. She'd stepped closer to him for privacy, and with his height, he could murmur directly into her ear. "I'm still your dirty little secret."

His voice slid over her skin, hitting every sensitive

spot behind her ear, under her jaw, that deep voice that had said *sex* and *love*…and *mine*. She breathed in swiftly. Oh, what exactly had he said? Her body knew. She could've slid down his six-foot-two frame and melted into a puddle around his combat boots.

Her body knew. Her mind did not.

Tom put his patrol cap on. Pretty much every macho adjective fit the man: tall, dark and handsome, chiseled jaw, and yeah, he had six-pack abs and bulging biceps, because she'd seen everything that morning in Vegas. Dress all that up in a military uniform and she was pretty much lusting after the man she needed to divorce in twelve weeks.

He turned toward the doors. She clenched her own jaw against the sexual arousal and stepped back from Tom. He didn't need to know her secret weaknesses. She was a good soldier, a strong soldier, but around a man like Tom, she'd love to just surrender and embrace every feminine stereotype, to be soft and sweet and delicate, even fragile…

He turned back to her. "But you need to be prepared for your secret to get out."

Damn. She hadn't been expecting him to turn back around. She hadn't schooled her features into her army face. Her mouth was dry; she wet her lips.

He narrowed his gaze on her, eyes crinkling just a bit at the corners. Whatever he saw, it made one corner of his mouth lift in something that looked a little bit arrogant. He swept his gaze down her body and back up, as if she were standing there in silky lingerie instead of baggy camouflage and sturdy brown boots.

"You look good in uniform, by the way. Not fragile at all."

Fragile? It sounded like he knew what she was thinking. It was frightening, not knowing what this man knew about her. It made her angry as hell, too. "I don't care what I look like. What do you mean, I need to be prepared for my secrets getting out?"

That mouth that had kissed so generously lost its arrogant tilt and turned serious. "Someone is going to notice that we have the same address at some point, Helen. We're not making an announcement, but there are going to be questions sooner or later. What do you intend to say?"

She threw her hands up in frustration—and took another step back from Tom. Pheromones or sex appeal or animal magnetism, whatever it was, the man had it in spades. "This is the kind of thing I wanted to discuss in counseling."

"But instead we talked about fame."

With a sigh, Helen gestured toward the doors. "This is ridiculous. We might as well head out to the parking lot." She put her patrol cap on and beat him to the door to push it open herself.

In the setting December sun, he walked alongside her as if it was no big deal. "Your answer was better than mine. You used your fame for a great trip to New York, then decided it didn't need to exist after that. That's thinking outside the box."

She shrugged off the compliment. "Might as well get some fun out of it before you have to give it back, right?"

He gave her a look at that, such a look, she couldn't help but imagine Tom and herself having fun—very adult, conjugal fun—before they had to give that Vegas license back.

"I'm parked over here," he said, and that cocky lift at the corner of his mouth was back. "I'll see you back at the house."

Helen decided that was a very, very bad idea. "Oh— I'm going to— I've got to stop at the commissary and pick up some groceries. Do you need anything? Milk or bread or whatever?"

Don't say whipped cream, don't say whipped cream.

Why was she thinking about Tom and whipped cream?

"I'm good, thanks."

"Okay, bye."

She watched him walk away, feeling like a small creature that had managed to escape a big jungle cat. One thing was for certain: she might not remember why she'd married the man, but there was no doubt that she'd enjoyed the wedding night in a gold bed full of rose petals.

And he knew it.

Chapter Six

Tom waited for his bride to walk in the door.

And waited.

One hour turned to two. He told himself he didn't care. She was an adult, an extremely competent and self-sufficient adult, in fact. If she didn't want to tell him where she was, then he didn't care.

But he'd cared two hours ago. He'd cared enough to listen to a bunch of touchy-feely stuff about emotional intimacy. He'd cared enough to agree to let a counselor *facilitate* an *exploration* in the hopes of building a personal connection with Helen that had nothing to do with love or sex.

He chucked the remains of a frozen pizza into the kitchen trash can. Cardboard and crumbs, that was all that was left. Crumbs—he was begging for crumbs from his wife, for any little bit of his Saturday marriage that might be left this Friday.

I could have more.

When they'd stopped in the lobby, when he'd turned around and caught her staring at him…he knew that look on her face. Whether she felt emotionally intimate with him or not, she was attracted to him. She'd said that sex with him had made her remember something. If he *facilitated* that attraction, then their *exploration* of emotional intimacy might be unnecessary. If her memory returned, then all of the intimacy would return—emotional, romantic, sexual. They'd had it all. That was why he'd gotten down on one knee and proposed to her.

Dear God, he would have Helen back.

He hadn't married her for the sex, but if sex would jog her memory, he was game. Hell, he'd stand around in his own house without a shirt on and lick whipped cream off his fingers, if that would help. He'd already been thinking along those lines as they'd walked out of the lobby, because her desire for him had been as easy to read as a book.

He turned to place his glass in the sink, and there was her wedding ring, twinkling at him on the windowsill, mocking him. *You think you know her? You think you can take your shirt off and she'll fall into your arms?*

He'd been willing to try two hours ago. Tom looked at the clock. *Make that almost three hours ago.*

She was avoiding being alone with him. If he could read her, it occurred to him now that she could probably read him like a book, too. Had she known that *he* had known her desire for him was still smoldering?

Had she known that he'd already been thinking about starting a fire tonight?

Probably.

And less than an hour before that, when they'd first sat in the counselor's office, she'd looked frightened, and he hadn't been able to stand that. He'd nearly walked out of the session rather than see Helen afraid of him.

She was keeping a safe distance tonight.

He glared at the ring, then he glared at the clock. She was keeping a safe distance where? She wasn't spending three hours at the commissary, grocery shopping. She must have eaten dinner somewhere. The commander of III Corps and Fort Hood expressly prohibited service members from dining at restaurants in town while wearing their ACUs past 1900 hours. That was 7:00 p.m. It was past eight now.

Maybe she'd run into old friends and stayed to have a drink. She'd been in the army for eight years. It was inevitable for her to run into old friends from previous duty stations. That kind of thing happened all the time on every army post. But Helen was wearing her ACUs. No soldier could drink at an establishment off post while wearing ACUs at any time of day. Which meant, whether she was having dinner or drinks, whether she was alone or with a friend, Helen had to be on post.

That narrowed down the possibilities considerably. Given the military's clear distinctions between ranks, there were two bars on post. One was for enlisted soldiers who'd achieved the rank of corporal, sergeant or higher. The other bar was for commissioned officers, including captains like himself—and like Helen.

She was probably at the Legends Pub, then, once known as the Officers' Club. Enjoying herself. Catching up with old friends. Making new friends over beer or cocktails.

She wouldn't drive herself home. Driving under the influence could be deadly to everyone on the road. For MP officers in particular, it was also an instant career killer. Helen knew that. She'd call a car service or catch a ride with a sober friend at the end of the night. She could call him to come and get her no matter how much emotional intimacy they shared or didn't share. Did she know she could count on him?

Hours ago, Tom had changed into his usual lounging-around-the-house clothes: track pants and a T-shirt. He wasn't dressed for a night out, but he could drive by the Legends Pub's parking lot and look for her Volvo. If he saw it, he'd leave a note under her windshield wiper, something short and friendly that told her she could call him if she needed a ride. If he left now, he'd be there and back in twenty minutes, tops.

He nodded to himself. It was a good plan. The motto of the military police was *Assist-Protect-Defend*, and one MP officer should certainly assist another.

Especially because the last time she had a few drinks, she blacked out.

Tom turned on the faucet and started filling his glass with clear water, remembering the Vegas bartenders filling glasses with clear vodka, clear gin, the showy ways they'd flipped bottles over their heads. God, he and Helen had thought it was all so fun. But they'd enjoyed the show as they'd each had one vodka and tonic at that bar. One.

For the first time, it hit him: Helen hadn't had that

much to drink in Vegas. He'd been with her the entire time. She'd had less to drink than he had.

Why hadn't he thought of that sooner? Helen must be extraordinarily susceptible to alcohol's effects. Some people were like that, born with a metabolism that was off, a liver that didn't neutralize the alcohol at the normal rate. What if, even with only a drink or two, Helen became too incapacitated to make good decisions?

He drank the water in one slam. Helen was all grown up. She knew her limits by now. She'd be fine.

Tom told himself that as he stared at her wedding ring so hard his vision blurred.

He shook his head sharply, vision clearing as he stalked toward his bedroom to change into jeans and stomp into his cowboy boots.

Assist-Protect-Defend blurred too easily with *Love-Honor-Cherish*. Put them all together and it meant one thing: he was going to spend the evening at the Legends Pub.

With his wife.

"And then he said, 'I'm the sausage king of Chicago!'"

Every woman in Helen's circle squealed, laughed, shrieked and generally fell on each other in hysterics.

It had been a pretty funny story, the funniest one yet. They'd been shooting pool and telling tales of past dates from hell. Helen raised her glass in a toast. "Ladies, I think we have a winner. To the sausage king of Chicago."

They all clinked glasses and only two of the five of them spilled a little bit of their drinks while doing so. Unfortunately, Helen's friend Lizzy was one of the two who spilled hers, and since she had her arm around Helen's neck, it was Helen's ACU trousers that caught the frozen piña colada. Helen stomped her boot to shake off the slush. At least nobody had spilled anything on the green felt of the billiards table. Yet.

Lizzy was a captain in the transportation corps, same rank as Helen, different branch within the army. She'd also been Helen's next-door neighbor for a while at Joint Base Lewis-McChord. She'd been moved by the army to Fort Hood over a year ago, so Helen had been happily surprised to run into her here at the officers' pub. Lizzy had come for a Friday night out with two friends, also captains, who were rapidly becoming Helen's friends, as well. Lizzy and her friends had dressed for the night in civilian clothes. About half of the bar was in uniform, half in civvies.

The fifth woman was a lieutenant rather than a captain, her rank easy to know because she was still in her ACUs, like Helen. The lieutenant was younger than they were by a few years—okay, by seven or eight years—but one of Lizzy's friends had been the lieutenant's instructor at her Basic Officer Leadership Course, so all four of the captains had decided to "mentor" the lieutenant tonight.

Young Chloe was still in her first year as an officer, and she was having the time of her life, basking in the free beers they'd provided. Captains' salaries were higher than a new lieutenant's by a couple of thousand each month, so they were picking up the tab for their new mentor-ee. Chloe's enthusiasm was contagious. She was also basking in the sisterhood, if Helen guessed correctly. Women were so greatly outnumbered in the military, it was always a treat to spend a girls' night out with girls who'd also raised their right hands and pledged to uphold the Constitution with their lives.

But hands weren't being raised tonight. Glasses were. Lizzy's friend Michelle raised hers and proposed another toast. "Here's to all the sausage kings of all the lovely cities where we've ever been stationed. May they all join a monastery and never subject another woman to their craziness again."

"Hear, hear." Lizzy thumped her pool cue on the floor.

But Michelle wasn't done yet. "And here's to our future husbands. May they have the good fortune to find us and start sweeping us off our feet *soon*!"

Helen raised her glass with the rest. *But don't marry him just because you think it's time to get married.* She'd had months to wonder how she'd been so foolish as to marry Russell when she clearly hadn't been ready for marriage. According to Russell, she would never be. So why had she said *I do*? More and more, she was beginning to think she'd married him because he was the man she'd happened to be dating when her peers had started pairing off and it was time to think about settling down.

"Listen to me, Helen. Listen. Listen to me."

"I'm listening." Helen picked up Lizzy's arm and moved it to rest on Helen's shoulder instead of choking her neck.

"Don't be sad about Russell. We're drinking to the better guys we're going to find. I can tell you're thinking about Russell. He wasn't good enough for you. I'm glad you divorced him."

He divorced me.

But Helen smiled. "Thanks."

"You'll get married again, Helly. I know you will."

Already beat you to that.

Mrs.—Stroke.

Tom—Stroke.

Cross.

If she was only going to have one memory from Vegas, she didn't know if that one was a blessing or a curse. It didn't tell her why she'd married the man after the hard lesson she'd learned with Russell. It only made her feel hot and bothered. Good Lord, Tom could kiss. And he could...move. Maybe she'd married him just to sleep with him. Would she have been such a Puritan about that? Would she have demanded a ring and a license before sleeping with the guy?

How silly of her. This was the twenty-first century. She should have just jumped into bed with Tom Cross. And stayed there. All day. All night.

"What are you giggling about?" Lizzy asked with coconut-scented breath.

"Me? Giggle?"

"Yes, you."

"I'm just having a good time." Helen deposited Lizzy on a stool and started racking up the balls for the next game. Stripes, solids, the black eight ball. She fit them all into the triangular frame as an even more incredible point came to her: if she'd demanded a ring and a marriage, then Tom must have wanted to have sex with her very badly to agree.

Ha. If that were the case, she'd love to rub Russell's

face in it. Russell had said she was attractive *for a soldier*. As if she only cleared some lower bar for beauty. As if she couldn't hold her own against…whom? Civilians? Supermodels?

Helen pushed the triangle full of pool balls to the proper spot on the table. She leaned over to keep her hands on the triangle frame. "Okay, ladies. Are we ready?"

The women debated who should play this round. Helen silently debated whether or not Russell had been right or had been an idiot. The fact was, Tom Cross had married her, and it was possible that he'd done so because he'd found her so attractive, he'd married her just to get her in his bed.

But probably not. He could have gotten a woman for the weekend easily. Tom was hot. No matter how much Helen drank for the rest of her life, she didn't think she'd ever forget the way Tom had looked Sunday afternoon as he'd tied that white towel around his waist, the way it had left a slit up his thigh. Not that Russell was ugly or anything. He had a good body. He was in his twenties, and since he was in the army, he was physically fit. Nothing to complain about. But Russell was no Tom Cross. *That towel*…

"Here we go." Helen lifted the frame, leaving the balls in their perfect formation. Then she lifted her gaze, and there was Tom. In the flesh.

He was leaning against the wall, drink in hand, looking like heaven in well-worn blue jeans, with that talented mouth of his curved just slightly in a smile as he watched her.

She lifted the frame higher, so that it framed her face as she looked at him through it. She winked at him as she turned around to put the frame in the rack and retrieve her drink. *You're flirting. What was that? That was flirting.*

Tom pushed off the wall and started walking toward her. Had he looked good all week in uniform, in the same baggy camouflage pajamas she was still wearing? Yes. But she devoured him now with her eyes, head to toe. He was the reason God had invented blue jeans. A sacrilegious thought, perhaps, but when she'd gotten lucky in Vegas, she'd gotten really lucky. *I slept with that.*

He stopped just a little too close to her. An inch too close. "Are you having a good night?"

"Yes." She swallowed. "And you?"

"Better now. It got lonely at the house without you."

That wasn't what she'd been expecting him to say. It was too personal. It made her sound important in his life. In his home.

It wasn't flirting. It was…emotionally intimate.

I don't know you. Back off. You're gorgeous, but I was just flirting.

They weren't on the same page at all. He wanted her to act like a wife. She'd only wanted to wink at him, a cute guy at a bar.

Tonight's girl posse surrounded him.

"Well, hello." Lizzy actually batted her eyelashes at him.

"Who are you, and are there more of you?" Michelle made a show of counting the women. "There are five of us. We need five of you."

"Hello, ladies." Tom seemed more amused than overwhelmed. He looked at Helen and did the eyebrow-lift inquiry thing. *How are you going to introduce me?*

Good question. He'd told her to be prepared, hadn't he? Yet she wasn't. She had to wing it. "Everyone, this is Tom Cross. My...my roommate."

"Your roommate?" Lizzy and Michelle repeated in unison, their tones of voice sounding like that was an unbelievable description. Or like she'd won the lottery. Hard to tell.

"Yes, Tom's letting me crash in his spare bedroom until I can get my own place."

There. She'd come up with a perfectly true explanation. Except Tom wasn't letting her stay. He'd been ordered to share his house with her by a full-bird colonel.

Lizzy stared at him a moment longer, then snapped her fingers. "Chloe. Chloe, where are you?"

"Here, ma'am."

Chloe had been standing next to her the whole time. Lizzy threw her arm around her shoulders. "Very important lesson here, my young apprentice. Very important. If you ever, ever have him for a roommate, and he's just a roommate? You call me. I'll be right over. You got it?"

"Yes, ma'am." Chloe was really cracking up. "But it won't happen. Captain Cross is my company commander."

Helen set her drink down. The army was such a small world.

"Your CO? Oh, what a total buzzkill." Lizzy stood up straighter, making an effort to appear slightly more sober, and toasted Tom. "I get to finish my drink each time I make an embarrassing comment."

"How are you doing tonight, Michaels?" Tom asked Chloe. Or rather, Captain Cross asked Lieutenant Chloe Michaels, who apparently was in charge of one of the four platoons that made up Tom's company.

"Having a good time, sir. Friday night, and I'm not on duty."

Tom turned to Helen. "Are you corrupting my newest platoon leader?"

Helen held up her finger and thumb, indicating an inch of space. "Maybe just a little."

"Some roommate you are."

Chloe handed her pool cue to Michelle. "Play my next shot for me, ma'am. I'll be back in a minute." She left, drifting off in the general direction of the restrooms.

Smart girl. Even in a casual setting, command structure existed. It was less awkward for everyone if she just skipped out until Tom had finished talking to his peers about whatever it was that had prompted him to come over.

I am what prompted him to come over.

He'd come to spend time with her. Helen savored that little thrill as she looked at him. It was entirely too sexy that she had to look *up* at him. "Do you always come here on Fridays? I hear it's their busiest night. Saturday, I'm told, it's a ghost town."

Lizzy had herded the other women back to the pool table, giving Helen and Tom a little *alone time.* Helen had come here tonight specifically to avoid *alone time* with Tom, but now that he was here, wearing those jeans, she didn't see the harm in a chat. The bar was noisy, the bass voices of the mostly male crowd mixing with the bass of the rock music played by local musicians, all in bizarre juxtaposition to the childish snowman decorations that had been hung by the neon beer signs, in case they all forgot it was December.

"Not many Fridays. I just came over to say hi and to buy you a drink. What are you having?" He picked up her drink and took a sip. Behind his back, Michelle gave her a thumbs-up.

Helen took her drink from him. Yes, they'd kissed. And yes, they'd done more than that in Vegas. But this was too much, to just help himself to her drink like they were…lovers. Which they weren't. Not anymore.

"Cranberry juice?" Tom's expression was friendly, but his eyes watched her a little too closely. "Just plain cranberry juice?"

"Yes, it's cranberry juice. I'm driving." All the joy drained right out of her. All the fun went out of the whole room. "You came here just to see if I was drunk, didn't you?"

His friendly expression didn't slip, not one bit, but he didn't answer her.

"You thought I might have another blackout, didn't you? Just hours ago, I told you and our couns—you and *Jennifer* that I'm not a heavy drinker."

"I know you're not. I was with you the whole time last Saturday. But obviously, even a moderate amount of alcohol can give you black-out episodes."

"No, it does not."

"Yes, it did."

She turned her shoulder to him, back to the game, but it wasn't her turn yet. "Go away. I'm none of your business."

"Oh, I think you are, my dear roommate. You most definitely are."

"Only for twelve weeks."

"Every single week that I'm with you, I'm going to protect you. I made a vow."

"Wedding vows don't say 'protect.'"

"Cherish. I'm going to make sure that someone I cherish doesn't black out anywhere unsafe or with anyone who might be unsafe."

She made a little scoffing sound, but in case he hadn't heard it over the music, she slid him a look, too. "You're a little late on that one. I already woke up in a stranger's bed last Sunday morning."

He barely showed any response, but he'd heard her. His eyes had widened just enough to give it away. She turned back to her game, but now Lizzy was talking to some guy in a flight suit. Girls' night was falling apart.

Tom stepped behind her, standing much too close. His fingertips rested lightly on her waist—there were rules against public displays of affection in uniform, so this was appropriately subtle. And effective. When there were only fingertips to feel, she felt each one. His mouth was close to her ear. "You were never unsafe with me."

Oh, that voice. That damned voice that triggered an instant arousal, every damned time.

He was a jungle cat, purring in her ear. "You were never, and you will never be, unsafe with me. You know that, Helen. Deep down, you know that's true. It's why you made love to me on Sunday, isn't it?"

He was probably right. He'd looked so incredibly handsome, he'd kissed her so incredibly beautifully, and she'd known, deep down, it would be safe to have sex with him. So she had.

Here in the crowded pub, with his warmth at her

back and his fingertips on her waist, she could imagine how easy it would be to give in to that attraction again.

Then afterward, he'd caress her face and call her *dream girl* and expect her to feel some lifelong commitment to him. He would expect to have a say in her life, to control the steering wheel and choose the highway and decide whether or not she'd eaten enough and slept enough.

Twelve weeks. She could resist him for twelve weeks.

She stepped out of his reach and turned to face him. Keeping her voice just under the pitch of the crowd, she made him a deal. "You cannot follow me around for twelve weeks. I'll let you know if I'm going to be staying out late, so you don't have to worry about upholding any vows. I'll text you, and you won't come babysit me. Deal?"

He glowered at her in silence.

Silence was not an answer. "It's not negotiable. It's a deal whether you agree or not. I'll text you in the future. You won't follow me around like some creepy stalker for twelve weeks. That's it. That's how it's going to be."

"There's one problem with your plan."

Helen chalked her pool cue and gave him her best version of his eyebrow-raised-in-question.

"It won't be for twelve weeks." He stepped close to her once more and used his entire hand on her waist to keep her in place as he spoke very deliberately into her ear. "I made you a vow. I will never divorce you. If you want to divorce me, you'll have to live here for six months before you can break the promises you made."

He let her go, nodded to Lizzy and Michelle, and walked away.

"Oh, my God," Lizzy said. "You are so lucky to have him for a roommate."

Chapter Seven

"If a genie appeared out of a magic lamp and granted you three wishes, what would they be?"

Tom scowled at Helen.

She shrugged and pointed to the card in her hand, her body language clear: *I didn't write the question.*

So Tom scowled at their counselor as she sat at her desk. "Are these questions supposed to be taken seriously?"

"It's up to the two of you to read whatever you like into the questions," Jennifer said, her tranquil, even tone grating on his nerves.

Wish number one: I wish Helen would stop hiding in her bedroom when I'm in the house.

Tom was not in the mood for this. This week's session was on Wednesday instead of Friday, so it hadn't even been a full week since their first session with its whopping two questions. But the five days had been long. After Friday night's debacle at the Legends Pub, Helen was so damned quiet in her room—in his spare room—that he'd looked out the window at the driveway just to see if her car was there, so he'd know whether or not she was in the house. He never heard her playing music. He never heard her watching a movie on her laptop. He never heard her footsteps on the hard tile of the sturdy, single-story house.

It took the silent treatment to a whole new level. He'd always known when Dad was in the house, that was for damned sure. What good was giving someone the silent treatment if your target didn't know you were in the same vicinity, ignoring them?

His father would make a point of reading the newspaper at the kitchen table when Tom came home from practice.

Hi, Dad.

A turn of the newspaper page. Silence.

Tom would know he was in trouble. He wouldn't always know why. And when he was sixteen, he'd dared to ask: *Is there some specific reason you can't hear me today?*

Dad had turned the page again. There was no way he'd read the pages already; that had been his answer to his son, his only son, who wasn't worth speaking to. After all, at age sixteen, Tom wasn't a fighter pilot. To his father, fighter pilots like himself were the elite. They deserved respect. The rustle of the paper was all Tom deserved. And that day, Tom had been angry, done with it all.

Guess your hearing isn't what it used to be. Too many jet engines got you after all these years, Colonel?

Dad had launched himself out of the chair and Tom had instinctively backed away until he was flat against the wall, scared spitless. At sixteen, he'd been as tall as his father, but still lanky and lean. Dad had been— hell, he might not even have turned forty yet—all mature muscle, and he'd been so for a couple of decades. Dad could have kicked his ass, and they both knew it. "You think I can't hear you, son? You think that I can't hear you? Do you, boy?"

Tom hated when Dad's spittle got in his face, but he knew not to turn his face away. Dad expected you to look him in the eye while he told you why you sucked.

The really sad lesson Tom had learned that day was that spittle and screaming were preferable to the silent treatment.

I wish my wife would talk to me. Yell at me. Whisper to me. Stay in the same room that I'm in for more than thirty seconds.

Her wedding ring was still on the kitchen window-sill.

"Three wishes?" she prompted him.

"Fine. I'd wish for a million dollars, world peace and three more wishes."

"You're not taking this seriously."

"And you are?"

She looked nervous for one moment, then hid it smoothly. "Okay, let me think what I would wish for. Seriously."

Tom watched her tap her perfect finger on her perfect lips. At least her lips were moving during counseling. She'd been silent for five days.

"I'd wish…"

"You'd wish that you'd never met me." Pain made him impatient.

"You're wrong. I'd wish that I could remember."

Hope. It hit him so squarely in the chest, he stayed seated when he wanted to vault out of his chair and pull her out of her own. She wanted to remember him. "Helen—"

"I'd wish that I could remember, because you are so pissed off at me. You also have me at a disadvantage. You know everything. When I woke up in Vegas, you knew my occupation and you knew where I was going. You knew that I had been married, and what my ex's name is. It's terrifying."

"That's why you've been avoiding me?"

"I'm not avoiding you."

"Bull. C'mon, Helen. Nobody really lives in their bedroom after high school."

"I read a lot."

"Sit on the couch and read. Eat at the table instead of squirreling away your food in your bedroom."

"I don't squirrel away anything."

"You do."

"I'm not going to eat in front of you," she said, as if he'd suggested something completely out of line. "I cook and shop for one person. It would be rude to eat in front of another person when you don't have enough to share."

"We could eat at the same time. We could eat our separate dinners together."

"*Why would we do that?* We're getting divorced. Why should we start building a little domestic routine? Why should we build a—build the…"

"Build emotional intimacy?"

Helen fell silent.

Tom looked at Jennifer. "That's why we're here, isn't it? Emotional intimacy?"

It wasn't the kind of intimacy he had in mind right now. He'd like to haul Helen off to bed, frankly, where they could screw their brains out until she remembered the pleasure and he forgot this pain.

Jennifer sat placidly, hands in her lap, and gave Helen a schoolteacher's patient and encouraging nod. "Three wishes?"

Helen tossed the card down onto the table. "Fine. So first, like I said, I'd want to remember everything in Vegas, so I would know what I did and how to undo it."

Yeah, yeah. Divorce. Got it.

"Second, I'd want…a fresh start. I want to start over with everything. A new place to live, new furniture, new everything. And this time, if I don't love it, I won't settle for something that's only adequate."

Tom nearly vaulted out of his chair again. She remembered! She didn't know she remembered, but that was the conversation they'd had while waiting at the chapel, minutes before they'd said *I do*. She remembered. Sort of. Subconsciously.

"And for the third wish…" She tilted her head, studying him. "World peace."

Smart aleck. *His* smart aleck, who was still in sync with him.

Tom was still amused with world peace as he drew the next card. "How would you describe me to someone else?" He looked over the edge of the card at Helen. She knew he was thinking of the pub, and he knew she was thinking of the pub.

In unison, they answered: "Roommate."

He tossed the card onto the discard pile. This was going well, far better than he'd expected. Helen had remembered something, even if she didn't realize it. Plus, they'd just added a shared memory of something new, the night he'd met her friends at the pub. It all felt like progress to him. Helen was trying to remain serious, but she was failing. A smile toyed with the corners of her mouth.

She drew the next card, and the smile died. "Have you ever cheated on a romantic partner?"

"No."

She looked skeptical. "Never? Not even in high school or college?"

"Never."

"So, if you were sleeping with a girl in college, you would break up with her before sleeping with someone else?"

"Yes. But just to be clear, I didn't jump out of bed with one girl on Monday, tell her goodbye and jump into bed with a different girl on Tuesday."

"How would you do it, then?"

"Do what? Find a new girlfriend in college?" He shrugged. "If I broke up with a girlfriend on Monday and saw someone else I wanted to get to know on Tuesday, then I'd ask the new girl if she wanted to get coffee or something. Maybe go to a party that weekend. Maybe a movie, if I could scrape together the money. That ROTC scholarship was the only way I could afford college. Money was tight." *Dad was stingy.* "I had to come up with cheap date ideas. Laying a blanket out on the college green to look at the stars was cheap."

Helen set the card down with a little shake of her head.

"I *dated* in college, Helen. I didn't just hop from mattress to mattress with any girl who was willing. I got to know girlfriends first, before they became… girlfriends."

Who suckered you into his bed for a one-night stand and then broke your heart, dream girl?

But Helen was silent. He hated the silence.

He filled it. "That's not the stereotype you're thinking of, is it? But I think most guys take the time to get to know someone before they start sleeping with them. Don't do that little scoffing noise. I'm serious. Most guys I'm friends with, anyway. Sex with a total stranger was never my goal, even in college."

"So that must have come later." She wasn't being silent, after all. She'd just been thinking. "Am I supposed to believe I was the first?"

"The first what?"

"You slept with me when you didn't know me. You jumped into bed with me the first day you met me."

Shock at the accusation kept him silent, just for a moment, but long enough for Helen to throw up her hand impatiently. "I'm just trying to figure out why you are so determined to spend six months with a one-night stand. You won't move on to the next girlfriend until you break up with me, right? You can be rid of me in twelve weeks. We only have to do this through Valentine's Day. But at the pub, you *informed* me it would be six months. You'll wait until I've lived here for six months, just so I'll be the one doing the filing. That's crazy."

She was intent on him now, speaking with conviction. "Twelve weeks from now, you could go file for divorce and sleep with someone new the next day with a clear conscience. What man wouldn't want that? I'm sure you have no problem attracting women. Michelle wanted five of you, remember? In twelve weeks, actually eleven now, you could have a woman on Monday, another on Tuesday, another on Wed—"

"Stop it." He hissed the words out through gritted teeth, startling Helen into silence. He pressed that advantage, sitting forward in his chair, on the very edge of his seat, slipping his knee between hers. "Nothing about us began as a one-night stand. I got to know you, Helen. I loved you. I married you and then we slept together. That's the way it happened. It was traditional, not anything as shallow as a one-night stand."

"You make it sound like we dated for months. How long did we know each other before the wedding? Eleven in the morning until just after midnight? Fourteen hours, max."

"Fourteen hours isn't better or worse than fourteen days or fourteen months." When he would have taken her hands, she withdrew them, folding them together to rest on her lap, very close to her body.

He would still say what needed to be said. "If you think I'm going to be tempted now by the idea of having a string of one-night stands, if you think for one moment that I'll agree to file for divorce in eleven weeks so I can do some guilt-free bed-hopping or whatever this thing is that you think I want, then you don't know what I want at all."

"Exactly. I don't know what you want. That's why we should get divorced as soon as possible."

"No, Helen. That's why we should keep sitting here, asking each other questions."

He drew the next card and pretended to read it. He

didn't really care what it said. He substituted a question of his own. "Has a romantic partner ever cheated on you?"

Helen exhaled, a little whoosh of air like she'd walked into a piece of furniture unexpectedly. At her desk, Jennifer exhaled in surprise, too. She knew that question wasn't on her card, but she didn't intervene.

"If you count a purely physical one-night stand, then yes, my first husband cheated on me."

"I count it." *That son of a bitch.* "You don't?"

She tucked her hands under her arms, keeping them far from him, or perhaps just holding herself against a remembered pain. "He told me about it. I never would have known. He said that the old cliché that it meant nothing was quite true. It was an accident. Wrong place, wrong time. He was on a TDY assignment, out of the state for sixty days. He said he hadn't had a one-night stand since we'd married, and that even though it was hard for guys to turn down a little no-strings-attached sex, he wouldn't do it again."

"That didn't cause your divorce?"

"It was so hard for me to even comprehend it. I was sure that marriage meant one type of behavior, which made it hard to conceive of him doing the complete opposite. He didn't tell me until six months after it happened, so it was almost like someone telling you about a dream they'd had. Not real. I didn't kick him out or anything after he told me about it, but we did go to marriage counseling. A couple of sessions."

At that, Tom sat back. When Colonel Reed had ordered her to marriage counseling, she must have been outraged at a different level than Tom had been. She'd already been through it once, and it hadn't fixed her first marriage.

"It was the second time he cheated that did it."

Son of a bitch.

"He wasn't out of town. I walked in on him in our house." She tapped her temple. "I've got that image stuck in my head forever now. My husband's bare backside in the air, going at it with someone else. The concept of him cheating on me suddenly got very, very easy to imagine."

She looked away, staring, unseeing, as she remembered something Tom wished she'd never known. Then she darted a glance at him and wrinkled her nose. "They were on my side of the bed. That struck me as deliberate. A slap in the face."

Enough. Tom didn't want to drag any more out of her. These counseling sessions were the only time he got to sit down with her face-to-face and really talk. He was sorry that any of his precious, limited time with her had to be spent recounting the tale of her cheating first husband.

He addressed their too-silent counselor. "That's enough. I think we've had enough for today. We can stop here."

"Certainly," Jennifer said. "Just as soon as you answer *your* question, we'll be finished."

"Have I ever been cheated on? No." He looked back at Helen and shook his head sadly. "No."

She nodded, briefly, his answer hardly affecting her as she sat apart from him, swallowed by deep chair cushions that were hard to get out of.

Tom almost wished he had been cheated on, just so Helen wouldn't feel so alone.

* * *

Helen washed her single bowl, her solo spoon, her one glass and put them neatly in the drainboard to dry. Diamonds and gold glittered at her as the evening sun came in the kitchen window. She wouldn't take ownership of that ring. Tom wouldn't take it back. She'd tried to persuade him at yesterday's counseling session, tried to remind him that the freedom of bachelorhood was within his power to regain within a matter of weeks, but he'd steadfastly stuck by his claim that he preferred to be…steadfast.

It made her heart hurt. Everything made her heart hurt, every encounter, every conversation, even the sight of that truly pretty wedding band. She couldn't take ten more weeks of this. There was no way she'd make six months. She needed a new plan.

She glanced at the clock. Tom wouldn't be home for at least fifteen more minutes. She remembered well how demanding a company command was. Now that she'd completed her two years as a commander at Lewis-McChord, she had a desk job in brigade headquarters, which seemed embarrassingly easy in comparison.

She was in charge of making contingency plans on paper. Tom was in charge of one hundred and twenty human beings with all their vagaries. To ensure every one of those soldiers could execute their missions, Tom had to do more than just oversee training exercises and qualifications. A soldier couldn't perform at his or her best if they were dealing with bankruptcy or had no child care arrangements, for example. The problems crossing a commander's desk were as varied as the human beings that served in the military—and through it all, every minute of every day, the commander led by example mentally and physically, demonstrating the right attitude, setting the right priorities, exceeding every standard on every task.

The days were long. A supportive spouse was a real asset to a company commander. Russell Gannon had not been that spouse.

I'm not that spouse for Tom, either.

She didn't need to be. She was a three-month roommate. Besides, Tom didn't need a wife to be a good commander. She probably would have been better off without a husband. She believed she'd been a good commander *despite* being married to Russell, not because he'd been any kind of support. Judging from the commendations she'd received, the army agreed that she'd done well. And now, perhaps as a little reward or a little downtime, she had a cushy desk job. Fortunately.

Her desk job enabled her to keep her life from becoming entwined with Tom's. Helen left promptly at 1700 hours, or five in the evening, immediately after retreat sounded and the flag was lowered. Tom didn't make it home for at least an hour after she did, often an hour and a half. That gave her a chance to take care of her dinner and dishes and laundry, so she'd be back in her room and out of his way when he pulled into the drive. She was the ideal roommate.

"Oh, my gosh. I've been doing this all wrong."

She turned her back on the wedding ring and paced into the living room. There was no trace that she lived there at all. She didn't leave a basket of laundry that needed folding over there on the coffee table. She never left a dirty plate on the dining table. She didn't hang her patrol cap on the rack by the front door.

No wonder Tom wasn't the least bit disturbed at the idea of having her for a roommate for six full months. He never saw her, and yet all his bills had been cut in half. She was going to pay half of the rent, half of the electricity, half of the internet. Who wouldn't want to keep an invisible roommate like that for as long as possible?

Living with her needed to be so awful he'd go running to the courthouse the day those twelve weeks were up.

She needed to become the roommate from hell.

She turned in a slow circle in the living room. It was a bachelor pad, arranged around a large television and dominated by a black leather couch, but it was clean and neat. Orderly. Uncluttered. There wasn't even a single crumb on that black leather.

The man was a neat freak, then. It would be easy to drive a neat freak batty, wouldn't it?

She turned on the television for the first time since she'd moved in. It was tuned to a sports channel, exactly as Tom had left it. She flipped through the guide and chose the sappiest chick flick she could find.

She left the television on, girls weeping over wedding gowns, and left for the store. A bag of messy, crumbly, orange-dusted cheese puffs was calling her name.

Chapter Eight

"Have you seen the new captain at brigade S-3?"

Tom stopped short. He'd just been about to walk into his own office, where his four platoon leaders had already convened for their weekly meeting, their last task before they could go home for the day. He listened beside the door, an eavesdropper in his own company.

"If you mean who I think you mean, hell, yeah."

That was Salvatore, a lieutenant who was single.

"Hard to miss her."

And that was Phillips, who was married.

"I heard she's divorced."

Not yet, she isn't.

"Is she or isn't she? Does she have a wedding ring?"

"No, but not everyone does around here. Safety hazard."

"Well, yeah." Phillips laughed. "It's hazardous for

your health to make a move without knowing if someone is married or not."

"No, I mean rings are a safety hazard," Salvatore said. "When I was in ROTC, I saw this one cadet jump out of the back of a truck, catch her ring on a wood slat and have the flesh torn right off her finger. She was left with this bone sticking out. It was disgusting. We had to pick up the skin coating."

"Gross."

"One of the cadre had a Big Gulp in his vehicle. We dumped out the soda and kept the fleshy part of her finger on ice until she could take it with her in the ambulance."

"That is so sickening. Where do you get these stories?"

That was Chloe Michaels, his wife's little Friday night mentoring project. Tom waited for Chloe to give her peers the scoop that the S-3 was their commander's roommate.

She didn't. Whether she was being loyal to him or to Helen, she was obviously not going to be the one to spread the current gossip, not even accurate gossip. What happened at the pub stayed at the pub, he supposed.

Thane Carter, Tom's most senior platoon leader and executive officer, steered the conversation back to army business. "That's why they changed the regulation last year, allowing soldiers a single tattoo on one finger of one hand. Basically, they endorsed wedding ring tattoos. Soldiers were getting them, anyway, especially if they're about to deploy to somewhere they might see action. Nothing to get stolen overseas. Nothing to catch on a wood slat. That was a soldier-driven change in the regulation. A tattoo ring is smart."

"Only if you're sure you'll never, ever get divorced, and what are the odds of that in the army?" Salvatore asked. Then he must have realized only three of the four were single. "Besides your marriage, Phillips. I mean, you can get a tattooed ring. You'll beat the odds."

Tom let the silence last a moment. It said something about military life that even young, single officers were aware that if they ever got married, their relationship would face unique strains in addition to all the usual things that could tear apart civilian couples.

As Tom walked into the room, the lieutenants came to their feet. At age twenty-seven, Tom was both the oldest and the highest-ranking. He'd been deployed twice to combat theaters. He'd seen firsthand the flurry of divorces that seemed to happen within the first few months after the unit returned. Still, he'd bought no ring in Vegas for himself, because he and Helen had planned on having his wedding ring tattooed permanently on his finger. If he skipped the gory, combat-related reasons why ink was practical, then that left the fact that it was permanent. He wanted one because he liked the very permanence of it.

He'd sketched it out on the back of a cocktail napkin. Helen's name lent itself to block letters really well, HELEN-HELEN-HELEN. She'd loved his design.

He sat, so the lieutenants sat. As Thane started running through the roster of soldiers who'd requested leave for the upcoming Hanukkah, Christmas and New Year's holidays, Tom glanced at his bare ring finger. Helen's name should have already been wrapped around it, in ink, forever. Forever hadn't scared them. After all, she was army, too, so they were going into this with eyes wide-open. They understood the demands. His marriage wasn't going to fall apart no matter how much distance or time separated him from his bride.

He'd had no idea what was in store for him the morning after his wedding.

If you had three wishes...

If she remembered Vegas...

She thought if she remembered, she'd know how to undo things. She was wrong. If she remembered, there'd be no divorce, because she'd be as crazy about him as he was about her. They'd begin their married life with confidence: no divorce, no cheating—it wasn't in either of their natures. There would be a diamond ring on her finger and ink on his.

There would be love.

He didn't need three wishes. He only needed one.

When he got home, it seemed for a moment that his wish had been granted. His house was different. Lived in.

He had a wife, her hat by the door, her boots on the floor. Signs that she lived here; he wanted more.

Her car wasn't in the drive. When she returned from wherever she'd gone, she'd have to walk through the living room to get to her hermitage of a bedroom. He didn't want to miss her, so he stretched out on the couch, picked up the remote for the TV and waited for the chance to say, for the very first time, "How was your day?"

* * *

Tom's car was in the driveway.

Helen took her keys out of the ignition, took the groceries out of her back seat and took a very deep breath. This was it. Time for their living arrangement to change.

Roommate from hell. Roommate from hell. I'm going to be the roommate from hell.

She held the straps of all her reusable grocery totes in one hand and stuck the house key in the door with the other. It wasn't until she'd turned it that she realized Tom had left it unlocked for her. She walked in to the all-in-one living and dining room space and shoved the door shut with her butt. Not quite a slam, but not a quiet closing, either.

Her eyes went straight to him, a great big man, stretched out full length on the couch, sound asleep. Instantly, she felt guilty for slamming the door. She intended to drop the groceries on the dining table with a clatter, she really did, but she set them down gently— and looked at Tom some more.

He had one arm thrown over his eyes. Even in sleep, the muscles of his arm were carved in delicious curves. The man was pure eye candy. He wore a soft-looking T-shirt, a heathered navy blue. She'd better brace herself. That shirt was going to do amazing things for his eyes when he woke up.

She needed to wake him. Nobody would want to live for six months with someone who never let them catch a nap. She needed to push his feet off the end cushion and grumble that he was hogging the couch.

Or... I could just kick off my shoes and perch right there by his feet...and lie down, sliding up his body

*until I'm nestled next to him. The side of my face would
fit right in that warm space between the curve of his
neck and the bulge of his shoulder.*

She just stood there like an idiot, watching him
sleep.

*His whole body is really warm. I could just slip
right in there. Maybe he wouldn't even wake up...*

She didn't trust herself to sit on the couch at all.
Feeling genuinely grumpy, she marched over to the
couch and sat on the floor in front of it, facing the television, leaning back against the couch with a *thunk*.

Tom shifted a bit and peeked at her from under his
forearm. "Hi. How was your day?"

She had to look away from those blue eyes. Her
boots were still lying where she'd tossed them. He
hadn't felt any neat-freak compulsion to move them
out of the middle of the floor.

She scowled at the television. He'd put it back on
the sports channel, but it was muted. "I was watching something else, you know. I just had to run to the
Shopette and grab some stuff."

"I paused it for you and hit Record." He stretched
his arm over his head and felt around the end table for
the remote control. "Here you go. Hit this button and
you'll see the list of recorded stuff. There's your show.
You can un-pause it and pick up where you left off."

"Oh." She felt...she felt irritated. "I suppose you
want to watch the rest of this game right now, though."

"Nope." He hit the button to go back to her movie.
When he half smiled at her, she noticed his five-o'clock
shadow, the way his lips looked softer in comparison to
the bristle. "I'm not really invested in a cricket match

in Australia. That's one sport that puts me to sleep. As you just witnessed."

"Oh." She felt irritated at herself for having no other brilliant comeback than *oh*.

He turned up the volume for her. The characters on the screen resumed weeping over a wedding gown, gushing over its perfection, crying when the bride's mother advised her to enjoy every moment, for this was a once in a lifetime day. "You'll only wear a beautiful white dress once in your life."

Awkward.

Helen had worn a white dress twice. Not the same one, of course. The first one had belonged to Russell's mother. Both of Russell's sisters had worn it at each of their own weddings. It hadn't been anything Helen would have chosen for herself, but a Gannon bride was expected to wear Mother Gannon's dress, Russell had told her. She should be honored to be given the opportunity.

Oh, it's very generous of her to offer, but I'm not a Gannon. I'm a Pallas. Russell had been offended, certain that his mother's feelings would be crushed if nobody wore the gown she'd preserved for decades. *But she did see it worn. Each of her daughters wore it, right? It's a gown for Gannon girls. If you wanted to uphold the family tradition, then I think that means you would wear your father's tuxedo. The Gannon men's wedding tuxedo. See?* She'd tried to coax a smile out of Russell, but he hadn't been amused.

Helen had worn her mother-in-law's gown.

The white dress she'd grabbed from the shower in the Vegas hotel room had been something entirely different. The hem had been wet, as if they'd walked through a puddle, which must have been why it was hanging in the shower, but it had fit her like a glove. She'd looked in the mirror and fallen in love with it instantly. Then she'd picked up the damp hem, exchanged a few choice words with Tom, grabbed a croissant and run out the door.

"It's not about the dress, darling," the mother on the TV was saying. "It's about the man. Be sure, be very sure, that he is the one you want."

Yeah, well, Helen had screwed that up, too.

The movie went on and on. She wondered how much more Tom could take, because she wanted to run from the room, personally.

Tom just rolled on his side to face the screen more fully and settled in to watch, using his own arm as a pillow. What was wrong with him? He couldn't possibly want to watch this with her. It was terrible. The bride was indecisive, wondering if the groom was really the right man for her. The movie mother told her that once she said *I do*, she had to stay committed. Divorce meant she'd be unhappy for the rest of her life. She started pointing out how miserable all the bride's divorced friends were. Divorce meant failure.

Can't argue with that. I failed.

Yes, Russell had been the one who'd slept around, but if their marriage had been stronger, it wouldn't have happened. He'd been right about the number of hours she put into her command position compared to the number of hours she'd put into pleasing him.

The first time was my fault, I will accept that, Russell had said. *But this time is different. An affair is just a symptom of how bad our marriage is, and marriage takes two. You broke your vows, too. You were sup-*

posed to love and cherish me, remember? Can you honestly say you've been cherishing me when you work twelve-hour days for months on end? Do you see the problem? I'd been promised love, but you weren't giving it to me. You came home tired every night, too tired for me. Too tired to do anything in bed besides the basics. Very basic.

Helen felt tired just remembering it all, just as tired as Tom was now. She wished she could just lay her head back on the couch, and maybe…and maybe Tom would just run his hand over her hair and not be mad at her for being tired after a day that had started before dawn.

Tom tugged gently on her hair, snapping her out of her reverie. Her misery. "Would you like to switch back to the cricket match?"

She glanced over her shoulder at him. He touched her like…like he was her boyfriend. Like he knew how she liked to be touched.

He was watching her, not the television. He smiled at her, just a little bit, maybe a little sadly. "Sorry to interrupt your thoughts, but you were frowning pretty hard. Do you hate the show?" He tugged her hair softly one more time and let go. "Is all that dialogue about divorce making you think about Russell?"

"Oh." She swallowed. Everything about marriage and divorce made her feel like a loser. She couldn't say that. Or she could, but she didn't want to say that, so she stared at the carpet.

"I hope it's Russell you're mad at."

It's myself. I wasn't a good wife, and now I'm not going to be a good roommate, either.

"I didn't say I was mad," she said, looking stubbornly at the screen. The idyllic church scene had begun, adorable little flower girls toddling down the aisle, wandering toward the pews and back to the middle like little roly-poly pinballs.

"You can't have any regrets," Tom said. "You've got to be better off without a guy who thinks one-night stands don't count as cheating."

She winced at that. There was too much emotional intimacy there, for Tom to know those details, to know what she specifically regretted.

She knew what she was supposed to say. It had been a learning experience. She'd grown as a person. Those were the correct, mature ways to come through a divorce. But what she'd learned was that it sucked to find out how much someone else thought you sucked, and she didn't want to go through that again.

On the TV, the chubby and cherubic hands of the little girls dropped rose petals on the floor.

"I kind of regret not talking him into having a child. I have nothing to show for two years of my life. Those last months…" Living in exile from her own house, relearning how to cook for one person in a spartan, subleased apartment. She shook her head at the innocent flower girls. "It wouldn't have been so lonely. I would have still had someone to love."

Tom was so still and silent, she wondered if he'd fallen asleep. She couldn't look at him. If he was looking at her with any trace of sympathy on his face, she might cry, and there was no counselor around to set a time limit on that. Although, surely, a man wouldn't want to live with a woman any longer than he had to if the woman cried all the time over some past relationship. Maybe she should weep loudly.

Yuck. She couldn't do that. She couldn't even pretend to sit around and mourn Russell.

She hoped Tom had fallen back asleep. Just in case he hadn't, she finished her thought, but just in case he was asleep, she spoke softly. "But it's just as well. Russell would have only lectured a child the way he lectured me. I suppose it wouldn't be very nice of me to have a child if I knew in advance I'd be giving him or her a lousy father."

"No, it wouldn't be." His voice was stone-cold. "If you can't give the kid a decent father, don't have the kid."

There was nothing sympathetic or sleepy in that quick, vehement answer. She turned to look at him without thinking.

He looked away. Now he was the one scowling at the perfectly fake perfection of the ceremony on TV.

"Do you…do you have a child?" As soon as she said it, she knew he didn't. That would have been something she'd have known before she married him, surely. But she didn't know how she knew. She'd known he was an officer in the army. She knew he didn't have any children.

"Of course not. If I did…" He didn't take his eyes off the movie, but he waved a hand toward the room in general, in irritation.

"What?" She mimicked his irritated wave at the room.

"Don't you think there'd be a child here if I had one?"

"Well, no. Most men don't have full custody."

"I'd at least have a photo. Some toys for the days I do get custody. I'd at least *try* to be a decent father."

"I never said you wouldn't. I said Russell wouldn't."

They both scowled at the TV in silence. Now the bride and groom, rather than saying their vows like a normal bride and groom, were having some big teary, soul-baring, secret-sharing session in front of every single person they knew. Idiots.

"You don't have to worry about Russell anymore." Tom's voice had gotten more sympathetic again. He was probably looking at her instead of the television again, but she wasn't going to peek over her shoulder to find out. "I know it's only been a couple of weeks since you got your final divorce papers. You worried about him so long, it might take a little while to adjust to the fact that you don't have to worry about him anymore. But he's history. You can leave him behind."

She could, but she couldn't leave the lessons she'd learned about herself behind. Tom needed to let her go before she made him as miserable as she was.

"This show sucks," Tom said. "It's making you unhappy. We should go back to cricket."

Out of the corner of her eye, she saw him picking up the remote, taking charge, deciding what she should watch. The fact that he was doing what she'd like him to do only made that mildly less irritating. "What if all the dialogue about divorce had me thinking about you, not Russell?"

"There's no sense in worrying about that, either. Not tonight. You can't change anything for months."

"Just a couple of months." But she was wrung out, and she didn't want to watch the stupid show, and he was right—there was nothing she could do about anything at the moment, on a Thursday night in December.

"But *months*." He sat up, two hundred pounds and

six feet two inches of solid male muscle moving grace-fully, making room for her. "So you might as well sit somewhere more comfortable than the floor while we go back to cricket and get baffled by the rules. I as-sume there are rules. It seems like the British would have made rules, right?"

He'd made the offer so casually, so perfectly, that she'd almost sat on the couch before she remembered that she was supposed to be difficult to live with.

She drifted toward the sloppy pile of grocery bags on his table. "You don't mind if I eat on the couch, right? I'll just eat these straight out of the bag so there's no dirty dishes." She held up the orange-powdered puffs.

Tom raised his eyebrows, both eyebrows, not in a question but in surprise. "Are you kidding me?"

Ha. Got him.

But he smiled like a kid at Christmas. "I love those things. If you let me help you eat this bag, I'll buy you two more tomorrow, I swear."

Chapter Nine

Helen was bad at being a bad roommate.

She hated being a failure at this. She hated being a failure at anything.

Almost a week of leaving dirty dishes in the sink, of taking showers that lasted so long that there was no hot water left for her roommate, of parking her car in the driveway so close to Tom's car that he couldn't get his driver's side door open—nearly an entire week of that had seemed to have no effect on Tom at all.

It affected her. Desperate to make him think six months would be too long to live with her, she'd resorted to the worst thing she could think of this evening. She'd baked chocolate chip cookies. From scratch. It would be torture to smell them baking and not be offered a single one.

She stared at the heavenly flat circles of butter,

sugar and melty chocolate as they cooled on the kitchen counter. Her household goods hadn't arrived from Seattle yet, so as a substitute for cooling racks, she'd helped herself to the grill rack off Tom's outdoor barbecue, unscrewing it with his flat head screwdriver and bringing it in to sit on the kitchen counter.

It hadn't inconvenienced him. Christmas was just a week away, and although Texas was a southern state, it was still too cold to hang out in the backyard and cook burgers.

The cookies were cooling on it now, smelling like heaven. She couldn't force herself to put them in a container and take them all into her bedroom. She wasn't that mean, and Tom hadn't done anything mean except refuse to divorce her.

She thrust a spatula under a half dozen cookies and threw them on a plate while the chocolate chips were still warm and melty. She put another half dozen on another plate and stalked into the living room, where Tom was watching one of her favorite shows on TV. Did he just happen to have the same taste she did in shows, or was this yet another thing he'd learned about her in Vegas? Was he using it against her?

She was trying to pull off an act as the worst roommate. What if the way he liked what she liked was also an act? What if she fell for it, only to find out the real Tom was as hard to live with as Russell had been? She wondered how long he could keep up this nice guy act before the true Tom Cross came out. She was having a difficult time maintaining her own act.

Maintain? Ha. She hadn't succeeded in annoying him yet. Now she was going to feed the man home-made cookies.

She handed Tom a plate silently, then stalked over to the dining room table and sat down with her own plate. When he said *thanks*, she shoved an entire cookie in her mouth. Anger-eating was a thing.

"When do your household goods arrive from Seattle?" he asked, using the standard military phrase for all-your-stuff-from-the-last-house-you-lived-in. "These are delicious, by the way."

She shoved another cookie in her mouth.

"I'm asking because you obviously hate my couch so much, you'd rather sit in a hard wooden chair. Maybe we can use your couch instead when it arrives. Move mine into the garage."

Russell's damned furniture was going to force her to work with Tom to arrange room to store it all. To cooperate. She'd have to put things in Tom's garage. She'd have to stand the futon vertically in a corner of the spare bedroom to try to fit her own bed in there, the bed Russell had used for sex with another woman. But it would be more comfortable than a futon, right?

Another cookie got crammed in her mouth, fat and carbs and refined flour, good for her tongue, bad for her body. She supposed she could line up a few shots of tequila instead—they could hardly be worse for her than the cookies—but if she woke up with no memory again, then she'd be as worried as Tom was that she had some kind of bizarre alcohol intolerance.

And why was she cramming food into her mouth? Because she was upset about furniture. She'd wanted a fresh start, a clean slate, but Russell had saddled her with the furniture he hadn't wanted for his own fresh start.

She really needed some milk to wash down these

cookies. She hadn't bought any, but Tom had a gallon in the fridge. A bad roommate would help herself, so she did. Then she poured a second glass and carried it out to the living room and handed it to Tom. His fingers grazed hers, skin warm against hers for less than a breath. With his tongue, he cleaned a cookie crumb off the corner of his mouth.

What was she supposed to *do* with him?

She stomped back to the table. What she wanted to do was cry. Ugly tears, runny nose, guttural sobs. Because she'd taken a detour to Las Vegas, her whole life had gotten twisted into a knot. She should never have deviated from the straight path she'd planned.

It had started perfectly. With the divorce papers in her hand, she'd gone to a salon and had her long hair cut into a bob. *Whose opinion is more important to you than your husband's?* Her own opinion was, thank you very much. She'd had a bob in college and liked it, so she'd had it cut that way again. When she'd headed her car toward Fort Hood, the road ahead had looked so clear: twenty years in the army, a retirement at age forty-one, followed by living on her savings to get a PhD, perhaps teaching college as her second career. Alone.

She was supposed to be alone right now. It was the best, least stressful path through life for someone like her. Someone who didn't partner well. Look how sour everything had gotten with Russell.

Tom laughed at something on her favorite damn TV show.

Look how awful she was at living with a man who thought he loved her.

But whomever Tom had fallen in love with in

Vegas, it wasn't her. *This* was the real her, shoving cookies in her mouth, incapable of crossing that line to total bitchiness, yet incapable of meeting Tom's expectation that they were soul mates.

Please, please divorce me after Valentine's Day. I can't live like this until June.

"Name something you like about your own appearance and explain why."

Tom hated these questions. They didn't feel intimate. On the other hand, they were the only reason he got one hour every week to sit and stare at Helen—and have her stare back.

"You go first," she said.

"I'm a guy. Guys don't waste a lot of time in front of the mirror."

"Oh, but girls do?" Helen was spoiling for a fight, pugnacious and pouting in her overstuffed chair.

Tom sat back in his. He slid one booted foot forward, in between her boots. Her calf muscles flanked his, one on each side. They'd first sat like this at a table beside a resort pool in Las Vegas, sharing a meal. Talking, then touching. Meshing together.

This was our first touch. This was the beginning. You weren't angry then, not one bit.

"I don't know how much time all girls spend in front of mirrors, but you don't spend much. You loaded up every square inch of the bathroom counter with all kinds of bottles and jars, but you don't use any of them."

She frowned. "How would you know? Are you spying on me in the bathroom?"

"They don't move. The labels weren't facing one

way yesterday, a different way today. They're gathering dust in place." *I'm not going to give you the fight you want.* "What was the question again?"

She scowled at the card. "Name something you like about your own appearance and explain why."

He glanced at his bare ring finger. If he'd gotten that tattoo, he could have said that was what he liked about himself. They'd been married eighteen days now. Only the kitchen windowsill wore a ring.

"You're taking too long to answer. You must know you have really, really blue eyes. I bet you were voted 'Prettiest Eyes' in your high school yearbook." Helen said it like an insult.

"Maybe I was. But before you get all pissed off about it, remember that, to me, they're just my eyes. Same eyes I've looked at in the mirror for twenty-seven years. I don't stand there and admire my eyes while I shave. I don't even notice them." He let his knee rock to the side, knocking her leg open. "I'm glad you like them. I think you like them. Either that, or you hate them." Another nudge. "Why are you so mad today? I love your hair, by the way."

"I—" She stopped in surprise.

"It makes me want to touch it. It's loose. Swingy. Most women in the army seem to either have short, short hair, or else hair long enough to scrape back and pin up. Yours is perfect. Not too long. Not too short. Just right."

"Like Goldilocks's porridge," she muttered.

He laughed. Another nudge. "What is making you mad today?"

Her gaze darted to the counselor. "That's not the question."

At the desk, Jennifer obligingly jotted down some notes and didn't intervene.

Helen sighed. "Why are you so *happy*?"

"You made me chocolate chip cookies last night. Who wouldn't be happy?"

She wouldn't be, apparently. She looked at him for one raw, unguarded moment, and he saw profound sadness in her eyes.

"You misinterpreted them," she said.

Did his smile falter? The sudden chill around his heart caught him unaware. "How does one misinterpret cookies?"

"I was baking them to make you unhappy, not happy." She stopped there and pressed her lips together.

"Well…" She wanted him to be unhappy? His voice was husky. His throat was tight. "Then in the future you need to know that they're my favorite. You're going to fail every time you try to make me unhappy with chocolate chip cookies."

"I'll fail." She tilted her head back to blink up at the unused ceiling lights. "Yes, I'll fail. I'd kind of hoped I'd be done failing this December."

Tom was lost. The only thing he was certain of was that Helen was blinking back tears when she blinked at the ceiling. He looked to Jennifer, to the professional counselor with the psychology degrees. Now would be a good time for her to use those degrees to step in and explain what was going on.

Jennifer had stopped writing, but she said nothing. The smallest frown marred her usual expression of polite interest.

Helen looked straight ahead once more, but that

didn't mean she was going to say anything else. She sat with one hand on each arm of her chair, posing like a statue of Abraham Lincoln, and just as talkative, damn it. Even a counseling session could be destroyed by the silent treatment.

You don't want to talk to me? Then I don't want to talk to you.

If the counselor was waiting to see who would speak first, she'd be waiting a long, long time. The walls came up, cold and familiar—but where had they been? When had Helen slipped right past them again? Had it been the cookies? The cheese puffs? The margarine mess that first night?

"Please explain how you expected cookies to make me unhappy." The sentence was forced, stiff and formal, through a throat that should have swallowed it.

He'd actually spoken first. Either his head had overridden his heart, or his heart had overridden his head, but either way, it was too late now. He'd done what he'd sworn never to do again, what he *hadn't* done again, not since he'd moved out of his dad's house: he was begging for attention from someone he loved when he—or she, now—didn't love him back. Begging for scraps. Crumbs. Communication.

Hell, he'd been doing that all week. He wanted the love of his life in his arms, sharing her thoughts, asking him about his. He wanted her in his bed. Instead, he'd eagerly caught the scraps she'd thrown his way, being pleased when she was just in the same room. Being happy when she silently handed him a plate of cookies.

"I wasn't going to share them." She swallowed hard. Maybe those words had forced their way out of her throat of their own accord, too. Not all the tears had been blinked away. They were still there, pooling in her eyes, waiting to spill over her lower lashes. "I was going to make your mouth water and then take them all into my bedroom and not let you have a single bite."

"Why?"

And then the first tears fell, although she sounded angry. "I've been trying to be the roommate from hell. A bad roommate. Didn't you *notice*? I tried so hard to inconvenience you—no, to *disillusion* you. Hogging the whole bathroom counter with all that makeup I hardly ever wear? What did you think that was about? That was about giving you nowhere to set your shaving cream."

"Why?" he asked again, voice hoarse, but it wasn't necessary. Helen's words didn't slow down. The dam had broken.

"I thought if I could be a bad roommate, you'd want me out of your house in February. But I can't do it. I'm not a mean person. I'm just feeling awful now, no matter what I do. I felt awful hiding in the spare bedroom and trying not to impinge on your space. I feel awful trying to take up all of your space. I feel awful when I make you happy, because it makes you want this fantasy version of me you have in your mind. I don't mean to set you up for disappointment over and over."

She stopped to suck in a breath that shook. "I was braced to make it to the end of February. We could be civilized and I could move out, but then at the pub, you said you'll never file. You told me I'd have to wait until June and file myself." Her tears fell in earnest. The agony in her voice cut through any of Tom's remaining walls as easily as a knife through butter. "I don't understand why you want to punish me until June."

"*Punish* you?"

"The only reason you won't file in February is because you made a vow to some fantasy woman who looks like me, but whom I don't even know, and you want to have the satisfaction of knowing you didn't break your vow. It's tearing me up to live like this, but you're going to put me through it, just to preserve this image of yourself as this noble man who keeps vows."

"It's not a punishment. I'm not trying to hurt you. My God."

"You're hoping for something to happen, but I don't have any memories miraculously coming back. I'm sorry, but I don't remember."

"That's because *you haven't tried*." The words came out on a wave of anger he hadn't known he was holding back. "You said you remembered something when we kissed, so now you won't kiss me. What's that tell you? There was a moment, Helen, the morning after. I called you 'dream girl' in that hotel suite, and you remembered for just a moment. I saw it in your eyes when you looked at me. And then it was gone, and you damn near ran me over trying to get out of there as fast as you could."

And now he was the one on a roll, words tumbling out in anger, thoughts he hadn't wanted to admit he had, not even to himself. "You could have stayed, Helen. You'd already remembered things twice in that half hour. You could have stayed and done like I said. Had some food, taken a shower, *relaxed*. It might have come back. I might have gotten you back." The pain was terrible, loving the same woman he was so angry with. "You didn't even try."

He realized he was standing. When the hell had he stood up? God *damn* it, he felt like a fool.

"I couldn't stay, Tom. I couldn't. I had to report to Fort Hood by noon and—"

"Did you really think the US Army was going to send out a national APB if you were three or four hours late? What was the worst possible punishment you think would have been leveled at you if you'd walked into Reed's office at fifteen hundred hours instead of twelve hundred?"

"I would have looked unprofessional. I wanted—I wanted my first impression to be good."

He laughed at that, completely unamused. "I don't know if it was good, but it was certainly one hell of a first impression."

Her tearstained face was killing him. He wanted to hold her fine jaw in his palms as if she really were that fragile feather. He wanted to run his thumbs down those tear tracks to erase them. But the last time he'd tried to touch her had been when her hands had been slippery with margarine. She'd shied away from him. She'd flinched.

He turned his back on her.

"Is he right?" Her voice was small. Quiet. She was talking to Jennifer, not to him. "If I had stayed that morning, would I have remembered everything?"

"That's impossible to say," Jennifer answered. "There are so many variables when it comes to memory recall."

A small pause. Helen pushed harder. "There must

be research out there. What is the science behind memory recall?"

Tom didn't trust himself to sit down again, but he turned his head to hear the counselor better. His heart threatened to pound too loudly for him to hear information that felt vital to the rest of his life. He forced his pulse to slow, to calm itself, like he did when he needed to pull a trigger smoothly and shoot accurately.

"The first factor affecting recall is that those memories had to have been stored in long-term memory in the first place. Certain drugs, including some abused for recreational use, specifically prevent memories from being stored. Alcohol may have an effect. Or if you'd sustained a concussion or other brain injury, the damage could have deleted the memory. If you don't remember, it may be because the memory isn't there to recall."

Another pause. Tom knew she hadn't been hit in the head. They hadn't touched drugs. Alcohol, though— that was possible.

"He says I remembered something for a moment when he said 'dream girl.' Does that mean the memories are stored there, somewhere?"

She was brave to ask. It took guts to find out one way or the other what the future might hold. She dreaded recalling something that he prayed she'd recall. He could not have asked these questions. He could not live without hope if the answers killed all hope.

"Again, there are so many variables, I can't make a guess with any accuracy as to whether or not you stored a specific memory. There are factors that we know make memories stick. Sleep is helpful. There have been studies conducted that proved students who studied material immediately before going to bed had better recall when tested the next morning."

They'd made love off and on all night long. The sun had risen when they'd fallen asleep. Maybe she'd slept five or six hours before she'd walked out of the bedroom with that petal-stained sheet wrapped around her like a wedding gown. Then she'd driven herself to stay awake for a solid twenty hours after that. Sleep was not in their favor here.

"Stress has an effect on both memory storage and recall."

As Jennifer discussed the effects in scientific terms, Tom closed his eyes against the memory of Helen's distress that morning. High stress, too little sleep, consumption of alcohol. Three strikes. His heart pounded beyond his control.

"Could I still remember now?" Helen asked. "You're going to say that's impossible to predict."

"To temper your expectations, I would say it's not likely. But there is no telling what might trigger a memory, or when. Have you ever had an odd experience where you catch, for example, an unexpected whiff of a candle, and you suddenly remember something you haven't thought of in decades, like candles on a birthday cake from kindergarten? Or you see an old toy and you suddenly remember receiving it at a long-ago party? Memories can be buried deeply and still spring back into our conscious thoughts, so I would never say never."

"But—but are you saying that two decades from now I might suddenly remember marrying him?"

"Well…well, no, I think that's unlikely. You first remembered our hypothetical kindergarten party the day after it happened, we presume, and then stored the memory. But in this situation, if you never stored the memory to start with…again, we just don't know. I wish the scientific community had more assurances for you, one way or another. I wish we had more time now, but I do have another appointment. Tom? Let's regroup now and wrap up for the day."

He needed time—a moment—he needed to keep breathing. His wife, the woman who'd held all his hopes and dreams, might never be more than a dream herself. She could be gone, forever. Would he forget her in time? Would he forget their first kiss? The way she'd said his name in the chapel? *I, Helen Pallas, take you, Tom Cross…*

Wouldn't it be easier if he let the memories grow dull? Then the pain might dull, too.

"Tom?"

"I'll see you next week," he said, polite words he forced out. He opened the door calmly and walked away.

He could not look back.

Chapter Ten

Helen wondered if she would see Tom this morning.

Their paths never crossed during the duty day, but this Friday, the entire brigade was participating in a unit run. They were in the same brigade.

They were in the same house, too, but she'd barely seen him since he'd walked out of that last counseling session. She wondered if this morning she'd have the chance to see his face, to hear him speak, to judge for herself how he was doing—how he felt about her.

Until that intense hour at the counselor's, she'd had no idea he blamed her for not staying longer in Vegas. For not *trying*. But why would she have tried to do anything with someone she didn't know? Why would she linger with a stranger when she had orders to report for duty? It hadn't occurred to her that she might have remembered if she'd stayed. Might have, Jennifer had said. Might *not* have.

Might never.

The possibility of *never* made her feel relieved. Tom was…a lot. A lot of man. A lot of heart. She didn't think she could handle being on the receiving end of so much love. She'd bungle it. She'd hurt him badly, and worst of all, he wouldn't be a snot about it, like Russell. Tom would really feel it. He'd be…isolated. It would be much safer for Tom if he gave up and moved on now.

Her thoughts tortured her even as she fell in line with the rest of the brigade headquarters company for PT.

PT, short for physical training, was so routine, Helen could go through it on autopilot. PT didn't distract her from her thoughts in the least, not after eight years of it. Across the US and at most installations overseas, Monday through Friday, soldiers stood in formation, performing whichever calisthenics the day's leader chose. Push-ups were a given. So was the side-straddle hop, which was just military speak for jumping jacks.

The most senior noncommissioned officer of the brigade, Command Sergeant-Major Richards, was leading the brigade headquarters company today.

"The side-straddle hop," he shouted.

"The side-straddle hop," the formation shouted back, including Helen, who shouted, if not enthusiastically, then dutifully. How many times in her life had she shouted the phrase *side-straddle hop*? One million.

She glanced across the expanse of the parade field as she jumped, across the hundreds of soldiers who filled that field, catching flashes of reflective yellow on their black PT uniforms as they did their calisthenics in the dark. Nearly half a thousand soldiers wore black track jackets zipped up against the chilly Texas morning. Tom was one of them, somewhere.

She'd never missed PT with her company when she was the commander, but she was on brigade staff now. It had benefits. The brigade staff only performed PT as a unit on Mondays and Fridays. The rest of the week, Helen was expected to work out, but she had options. Hitting the gym with her headphones on was a luxury she savored. Tom, on the other hand, worked out daily in the predawn dark with his company, setting the example for newly enlisted privates by keeping the routine of young privates, showing them it could be done, and done without complaint.

"One-two-three," the command sergeant-major called, keeping them all moving in sync.

She jumped to the barked-out rhythm. The headquarters company was a strange mix of senior sergeants and commissioned officers who had many years in the service. It was a novel thing to have achieved the rank of captain with a company command behind her, and yet be one of the lowest-ranking members of a unit. She remembered now that it was somewhat relaxing to be the follower instead of the leader. She didn't have to think about where to go or what to do or how to get one hundred and twenty people there, doing it. She was only responsible for herself. When she was told to do side-straddle hops, she did them.

But this Friday, she wished PT were more challenging. She wished she could force her brain to think about something besides her memories, her roommate and her future.

It was the last Friday before Christmas. Since they were stateside this year and not in a combat theater, the brigade was being granted a training holiday. After today's PT run, there would be showers, breakfasts, then a return to the unit for payday activities—a safety briefing, perhaps a reenlistment ceremony for a few soldiers who had committed themselves to more time in the service, perhaps a commendation pinned onto a deserving soldier. The brigade would be dismissed, and everyone not unlucky enough to have pulled a shift as the duty officer, a prison guard or a law enforcement patrolman would be free to go home and enjoy an extra-long weekend.

But first, the run. Brigade headquarters lined up, sized up—tallest soldiers to the rear—and started out. Colonel Reed set an easy pace. The purpose of this run was team spirit, not a test of speed and toughness. Those were the purposes of every other run on every other day. Today, nobody was trying to see if a weak link could hang at a faster pace. This was supposed to be fun, a short two miles before everyone spent four days stuffing themselves with pumpkin pie. The NCO calling cadence for the unit threw in a few Christmas carols. Everyone chanted them in unison as their feet hit the pavement at the same time, left, right, left, right, jingle bells.

Helen suddenly realized she had no idea where Tom planned to be on Christmas Day. Did he have family nearby? Had he bought a plane ticket to somewhere far away? She tried to remember something about his family, his hometown.

Nothing.

Behind her unit, the battalion headquarters company ran to their own cadence, their own carols. Following them, each MP company fell in line: the 401st, the 410th, the 411th and Tom's company, the 584th. She was probably a quarter mile ahead of Tom. Her unit returned to the headquarters building first, of course, crossing the finish line and then standing at ease in their rectangular formation as all the other units ran in. Helen didn't look obvious at all when she craned her neck to look past the 411th for a sight of Tom's company.

For a sight of Tom.

There he was, running in front, his platoon leaders flanking him. He laughed at something one of the lieutenants said. He looked so—oh, he was *everything*. Handsome, never more so than when he laughed. Tough, not even winded by the two-mile run. In charge, running so confidently in front of a hundred other soldiers, as though this was no big deal, as though being a soldier was a piece of cake.

She missed him.

The thought took her by surprise even as her eyes ate him up, as if she'd been starving for the sight of him. It had only been two days since he'd walked so somberly out of their counseling session. But in those two days, he'd become scarce. Maybe he was just a busy company commander, but during the few hours he was at the house, he was so remote, it was as if he was a polite stranger she passed in a grocery store aisle. He stepped out of her way when she walked into the kitchen. He spoke very little.

And he didn't look at her. All the polite *hellos*, an

excuse me or two, were said as he looked away from her, toward where he was going next. She had not looked directly into those blue eyes since she'd told him the cookies weren't supposed to make him happy.

Since she'd cried because he wouldn't divorce her.

She'd reassembled his grill. She'd left the rest of the cookies in a container on the counter, but he hadn't eaten another one, as far as she could tell. She'd picked up her tote bags and books and boots and everything she'd left out, then put it all away neatly in the spare bedroom.

If Tom noticed, he didn't say a word. He was sad because she might never remember their wedding. She knew that. He was sad; she was relieved. It had been a scary prospect, to remember being part of something as intensely emotional as Tom made it appear to be. Now, the pressure was off. Tom no longer watched her with those hungry eyes. He no longer watched her at all.

She hadn't expected to miss it.

A command was shouted, *Quick time—march*, and the 584th stopped running and fell into a regular march, walking—striding, really—straightening up their lines as they approached the spot where the brigade commander was standing with the American flag beside him. His staff stood behind him, including herself, two rows back.

Then it was Tom's voice calling the commands, in a voice meant to carry, like a quarterback calling a play to his team. "Eyes—right." One hundred soldiers snapped their heads to the right as they passed by, marching in step as the first sergeant counted a cadence. As the commander, only Tom rendered a hand salute, his hand flat like a knife's blade, finger-tips touching the edge of his brow, blue eyes intent on the brigade commander as Colonel Reed returned his salute.

Then those blue eyes locked on hers. She felt the jolt all the way to her soul. Everything fell away, the soldiers between them, the noise of the marching and the barked commands, and they looked at one another like they were recognizing a piece of themselves in a mirror. *Oh, it's you.* The flashing and chiming slot machines, the drunken bachelorette party girls in their feather boas, the smokers and the card tables, all of it disappeared. She had to speak to him, this man on the other side of the casino floor. She had to find out who he was, but she'd gotten on the dumb glass elevator and couldn't get off until it stopped at some random floor. As it rose, she turned to face him and kept her eyes on his for as long as she could. Just before she was going to disappear from his view, he smiled, and she smiled, because she knew he was going to come and find her. She couldn't wait.

"Ready—front." Tom gave the command, dropped his hand and turned his face away from her, looking straight forward, leading his company to their spot on the parade field.

An open field on an army post. Not a casino. A commander's serious salute, not a smile.

But the same blue eyes. She *remembered.* They'd been at the same casino. What had happened next? How long had it taken him to find her? What had he said? Helen realized she was breathing hard, nearly panting, although they'd stopped running almost ten minutes ago. The officers to her right and left probably thought she was out of shape, unable to catch her breath, but she couldn't worry about that right now. She was obsessed with her memory, turning it over and over in her mind. They'd seen one another on the casino floor. That first sight of each other had been electric and then…

She knew nothing.

What had happened next?

Helen had plenty of time to mull it over. The brigade parking lot was packed because of the PT spirit run, so leaving to go home to shower and change was like leaving a concert or a sports game. She sat behind the steering wheel, remembering those few seconds when she'd first seen Tom, reliving it all in her mind as she inched the car forward, then stopped. Inched forward.

Should she tell Tom? It would get his hopes up. She could imagine his face, the way he'd step close to her. He'd kill her with gentleness, smooth her hair back and cup her head in his hand and ask, "Do you remember now?"

She did not. She only knew, for the first time since she'd woken up married, that she actually wanted to remember more. Dear *God*, it had been so exciting the first time she'd seen him. Exhilarating. Still scary— she'd known in the casino that her life was going to change if she spoke to him. Her life was going to have a gap in it if she never spoke to him, too. She didn't want to wonder for the rest of her life what might have been, so she'd talked to him later—or so she assumed.

Well, duh. You woke up married. Obviously, you talked to him later.

She inched her car forward. This traffic—she wanted to lay on the horn and tell everyone to move, but of course she could not. Every single car was driven by someone in her brigade. There was no anonymity on post. She smacked the steering wheel instead of the horn. It hurt the heel of her hand. She inched toward home.

Should she tell Tom?

Finally, she exited the parking lot and started cruising at a normal speed.

She couldn't tell him. It would change everything, and he'd try to make her remember more. He'd want the whole commitment, the bed of roses, the diamond ring. She didn't remember any of that. She only knew that she'd spotted a man across a crowded casino, and that first flush of attraction had been intense.

She wanted to see him again.

His car was not in the driveway. Her disappointment was as intense as that first attraction had been. Big highs, big lows. It was silly to have gotten her hopes up that she would see him at the house right now. Most days, he brought his ACUs to his office and showered there after PT. Today was not unusual for him. She wouldn't get to see him again until this evening, if she was lucky.

But she'd seen him this morning at the run, leading his company, saluting, fierce.

A shower. She needed a cool shower.

She used the garage door opener to walk into the garage, where neither of their cars were parked, and hit the button to lower the door. She kicked off her sneakers and took off her track jacket and hung it on a hook by the door into the house. She slipped off her black track pants and hung them up, too. She walked into the house in her underpants and black workout shirt.

Her underthings, like the uniform shirt itself, were made of quick-drying fabric, so she was in no rush to strip out of any wet clothing, but her hair had gotten a little sweaty during the run. She lifted it off the back of her neck as she walked down the short hall to the bathroom. She'd just take a cool shower and wash her hair and not, under any circumstance, think about Tom Cross tying a towel at his hip in a Las Vegas hotel room, not while the shampoo bubbles slid down her body.

A *cold* shower. She would not remember the perfectly sculpted male body that stayed hidden under his baggy camouflage most of the time. She would get naked and get wet, but she would not think about—

"Tom!"

He stepped into the hallway from the bathroom and froze when he saw her. He'd been drying his hair with one end of his towel, and the length of it fell down his front, but otherwise, he was gorgeously, gloriously nude.

"Tom." Her voice sounded breathy. Had she wanted to see his eyes? She had. Had she missed the way his gaze followed her whenever she was in the room, a hungry gaze, demanding? She had.

Well, he was definitely looking at her now.

"I just…"

She just what? *Think, Helen.* The muscles in his legs were as chiseled as the rest of him. He had sculpted arms, washboard abs—she knew that. She'd remembered his chest, but now she couldn't tear her eyes away from that hollow in his hip, the dip between but-tock and thigh, the defined quadriceps.

She raised her gaze. He was looking at her face while she looked at his body.

She swallowed. "I didn't see your car."

He moved then, just to toss the end of the towel over his shoulder. It still draped down his front, an over-size towel for a very big man. He put a hand on his hip, as if he wore an MP black web-belt and holster, as if his fingers were resting just above his sidearm. "My car's not here. One of my platoon sergeants lives in this neighborhood. I skipped the parking lot traffic jam and caught a ride back with him."

"Uh-huh." She let her gaze follow the trail of that white towel. Blue eyes, tan skin, white towel. Vegas. Glass elevator. *Come find me.*

"Helen." His voice sounded sharp, a little angry. "Helen, look at me."

She looked at his face again, that mouth, those lips, the way the muscle in his cheek flexed as he clenched that strong jaw. Those eyes. Oh, he was looking at her now, like he was hungry for her. She wanted to have sex with him, if only because he was sexy. She wanted that body. She wanted to be able to touch it, to take it, to command it for her pleasure.

She shouldn't. There was a good reason she shouldn't, if she would stop and think about it. It would hurt him, he was vulnerable, something like that, but then he cursed, a single crude word, and pushed her up against the wall, and it was beyond ridiculous to think he couldn't handle what she wanted to do to him.

His mouth was on hers, a hot kiss. Then his tongue swiped her lower lip, and she opened her mouth to take his tongue and suck on it for a moment, until he pressed her harder against the wall with a sound deep in his throat while she had his mouth captive. He was nude and she wore only panties, so their bare legs tangled. She felt those defined quad muscles against her own thighs, all the way up to her hip, to the edge of her underwear. Higher than that, cloth lay between them, but his body heat penetrated the nylon of her panties and her shirt, and she wished she were nude all over, too.

He granted that wish, kissing her hard, keeping her pressed against the wall with his thighs as his hands grabbed the hem of her black shirt and jerked it up a little roughly, breaking off the kiss to pull it over her face, over her head, then throwing it down the hall. He didn't return to kissing her but watched his own hands making short work of her running bra, his fingers sliding under the tight elastic and pulling it away from her breasts. The elastic didn't have much give, so it abraded her skin a little as he lifted it, and she lifted her arms, so he could get rid of the bra and toss it down the hall, too. Then his hands were on her breasts, warm palms cupping her, shaping her as she put her hand on the back of his neck and pulled him closer, taking another hot kiss for herself, gasping in pleasure against his lips.

She grabbed his shoulders, fingers digging in. There was so much muscle there, so much meat, she could dig in and hang on and not cause him any harm. He lifted one hand to her hair, but there was no gentle smoothing motion, no warm cupping of her head. Instead, his hand pushed her head back, so he could taste her skin under her jaw and down the side of her throat. He pushed her higher up the wall, so her breasts were level with his mouth for a brief feast on first one, then the other, and then he lifted her higher again, his hands on her waist, keeping her pinned against the wall as the top of her head brushed the ceiling. His breath was hot on her as he breathed over the nylon, teeth grazing over intimate parts, before he pressed her against the wall with his mouth, too, sucking hard, right through her panties. With one thigh draped over his shoulder and one palm pressed against the ceiling above her, Helen came—came against him, came apart, came undone.

She became aware, dimly, that her stomach was being kissed, then her breasts, her cheek as he lowered her. She was once more face-to-face with Tom, incredible Tom, when she felt his finger jerk her panties to the side, felt two fingers open her up, then felt his body, thick and demanding, filling her. He pressed his forehead into the wall, his breath hot on her neck as he moved, until he shouted a syllable that never became a word and surrendered everything of himself to her, his muscles flexing, body shivering.

Helen didn't care if she ever moved again. Her legs were wrapped around his waist; she didn't need her toes to touch the ground for as long as she lived. It would take too much energy to lift her eyelids. She didn't need to, anyway, for she knew exactly who was kissing her, his mouth gentle on hers now. She didn't know what to say or what to do or what to think, so she kept her mouth pressed against his as he carried her into the bathroom. She heard the water being turned on, felt the steam on her skin, and then Tom stepped into the tub with her in his arms, right into the stream of water. He kissed her cheek gently, her nose, her eyelids, as he let go of her thigh. When her toes touched the porcelain, he let go of her other thigh, and when she was standing under the water, he stepped out of the tub and left her there.

That dazed feeling couldn't last, of course. She returned to herself, returned to the world. She found her shampoo and thought of nothing but Tom as the bubbles slid down her body.

When she rinsed off and dried off and ventured back into the hallway, Tom was gone.

Chapter Eleven

So much for married sex being boring.

Tom flexed the fingers of his left hand. He wore no ring. She wore no ring. Their own marriage counselor said they weren't working at a marriage, because it didn't exist for Helen, and one of the basic tenets of marriage was that two people had to know they were married, damn it all to hell and back.

So much for the married part of married sex.

That left sex. All they'd had this morning was sex. Out of control, hot against the wall, leave you wrung out to dry, pure, physical *sex*.

"Merry Christmas, sir."

Tom looked up from his desk to see his admin clerk, a young sergeant, standing hopefully at his office door. Tom kept his door open at all times, same as Colonel Reed.

"What are you still doing here, Sergeant Schreiber?" It was early in the afternoon. The half day of payday activities had been over since eleven. The troops were free to enjoy their long weekend.

"Sir, I didn't want to leave if you still needed me for—"

"It's Christmas. Go. Be jolly."

"Yes, sir." He was gone.

Tom wasn't going anywhere. He'd volunteered to be the battalion duty officer today. Christmas Day, too. Why not? The battalion headquarters building housed the company headquarters offices, as well, so Tom could sit at his own desk and push paperwork around. Maybe he'd start the new year with an empty inbox. He didn't necessarily have to stay in the building at all. As long as he was available by phone, he could be the legal point of contact for any issues with the battalion while the majority of its service members were on leave. Tom had thought he might as well volunteer to take the Christmas duty instead of letting it fall randomly. Otherwise, an officer that had little kids at home might have gotten stuck with it.

I'd at least try to be a decent father, he'd said, sounding like a petulant teenager as he'd talked with Helen.

The idea of going to his father's house to spend the holidays was laughable, even though Daddy Dearest lived in San Antonio, only a couple of hours' drive from Fort Hood. Dad was a retired air force general. Once a general, always a general. He still signed documents with his rank. He was still given military courtesies on military bases. Lackland Air Force Base was the reason he lived in San Antonio, so he could still drive onto post to use the PX, the commissary, the medical facilities, but mostly so he could do all that while getting his necessary dose of the military butt-kissing he'd so relished on active duty.

Mom, as usual, lived where Dad told her to live. If Dad decided they'd retire in San Antonio, then Mom would say, "Yes, dear." If the old adage that men wanted to marry a girl like the girl that married dear old Dad was true, it didn't apply to Tom. He didn't want a subservient wife.

A fragile feather. That was different. Helen had been talking about sex, not the whole relationship. He was all-in when it came to Helen's wants in the bedroom. Hell, he'd practically shoulder-pressed Helen over his head this morning, so he could devour her—

"Merry Christmas, sir."

Tom looked up from the computer screen he wasn't looking at. One of the four platoon sergeants, Sergeant First Class Ernesto, stood in the door, holding a dish covered in red plastic wrap.

"You, too, Sergeant First Class."

"I got a little something here for you."

"You didn't have to get me anything." Tom attempted his old smile. "You know I didn't wrap up anything with a bow for you." Gifts were awkward, as a matter of fact, and had to be inexpensive and distributed evenly to avoid any appearance of favoritism. He really hadn't gotten anyone anything.

Including Helen. What did you give the woman who was counting the days until your divorce?

"Well, you know my wife, sir." Ernesto set down the plate. Under the red wrapping, perfect gingerbread men were arranged in a circle. "She'll bake something at the smallest hint of an excuse. For Christmas, she pretty much goes crazy."

"God bless her for that." Tom stood up. "You'll tell her I said so."

"Yes, sir."

"All right. You've been here two hours too long already. Go—and get your platoon leader out of here, too." Tom had a feeling his lieutenants were hanging around since he was still hanging around, but they should go. He was only staying because he was the battalion duty officer.

Bull.

He was only staying because he didn't know what the hell to do at his house.

He knew what he wanted to do at his house. He knew a dozen things he wanted to do with Helen at his house, in his hallway, in his bedroom, in the shower, on the floor. He could have Helen's body, memory or no memory. He'd realized that after their first counseling session, when he'd murmured something into her ear in the lobby, and he'd seen the arousal in her face. She'd run to the pub then, to keep some distance. For whatever reason, she wasn't running now.

Maybe he should. She'd said something else during that first counseling session, during that very first question about fame. *Might as well get some fun out of it before you have to give it back.* Could he do that? Could he enjoy pure sex with Helen, just for fun, knowing they'd be divorced by June?

He found a slit in the red plastic wrap, slipped his fingers in, took out a cookie. They weren't chocolate chip, but these cookies were intended to make him happy, at least. Ernesto's wife baked with love. Tom's wife baked out of frustration. Desperation. Misery.

I feel awful when I make you happy, because it makes you want this fantasy version of me you have in your mind. It's tearing me up to live like this, but you're going to put me through it, just to preserve this image of yourself as this noble man who keeps vows.

"It's not a punishment," Tom whispered to himself.

I don't have any memories miraculously coming back. I'm sorry, but I don't remember.

Stress-sleep-alcohol. That trio had obliterated his hopes for love-honor-cherish.

He couldn't do it. He wouldn't survive having Helen's body but not her heart. No more sex, no matter how incredibly mind-blowing they were together. He needed to protect himself better, because as it was, he could hardly stand looking at her and knowing that she would never remember. In fact, he'd been avoiding setting eyes on her, until she'd been in his line of sight at the brigade spirit run. To have sex with her now would be insanity, not when he was mourning the loss of her. She just looked like his wife, but she wasn't his wife. Stress, sleep, alcohol.

Doomed.

They were doomed, and now they were only surviving until June came and she could move out of his house.

Or February. You could grant her wish and give her a divorce in February.

He pushed his chair away from the desk, violently. He could file? Him? That he would ever stand before a judge and say he didn't want her was unthinkable.

But you don't want her. You want the Helen you knew at the chapel. You don't even know this Helen.

What he knew of her was this: he was hurting her. She was unhappy. If he cared for her, he'd let her go in February. To drag it out until June was, in her words, nothing more than his way to punish her for a memory loss she hadn't chosen.

His desk phone rang. "Cross here."

"Sir, this is Sergeant First Class Corning, watch commander."

The watch commander? That was the senior non-commissioned officer who ran the MP station, overseeing the MPs who were on garrison duty. One company in the battalion was always on garrison duty, fulfilling the same role on Fort Hood that civilian police officers performed in towns and cities. The watch commander oversaw the MP station itself, including the holding cells. For the watch commander to call any battalion's duty officer, there was most likely someone in the holding cells of a significant rank. At the very least, a first sergeant.

The brigade had only been dismissed a couple of hours ago. Which member of the leadership had already gotten drunk and gotten in trouble?

"Go ahead," Tom told the watch commander.

"Sir, we've got a burglary in progress."

For the love of— Which of the battalion's buildings was being broken into in the middle of the day? The barracks? The motor pool?

"At your address."

"Say again?"

"We got a 911 call from your home address, sir. Intruder, attempted breaking and entering. I sent Corporal Jones to pick you up—"

But Tom had already hung up the phone and walked out of his office, down the hall, long strides eating up the distance.

Helen. She was home. He had to get to Helen.

Corporal Jones came running into the building, sliding to a stop in the hall. He was on duty, wearing the black MP bulletproof vest, a loaded weapon in his holster, handcuffs on his belt. Tom wanted only one of those three things at the moment, the one that would hurt anyone who tried to hurt Helen.

"Sir! There's a burglary in progress at your—"

"Go."

The corporal turned on his heel and then Tom was running, they were both running, out the door to the patrol car that waited with its lights flashing. Tom didn't need a weapon. He'd use his bare hands.

Helen. Screw the memories and screw the divorce and screw February and June. Helen had called 911. Sexy Helen, angry Helen, tearful Helen, Vegas Helen, it didn't matter at all—Tom would kill anyone who hurt Helen.

Because he loved her.

End of discussion.

Helen was furious. Tom was going to be almost as furious as she was.

Helen couldn't believe she was standing in her own driveway—Tom's driveway—with two MPs and a man in civilian clothes who was loudly informing the world that he was a brigadier general in the United States Air

Force, and she, Helen, *that woman*, was unauthorized to be in the house.

He wanted her arrested.

Well, that wasn't going to happen. The first MP had arrived within sixty seconds of her 911 call. The second MP had been two minutes behind. She didn't know the private and the corporal, and she didn't think they recognized her, either. She'd only been in the brigade for two weeks, and troops in line companies didn't work directly with brigade staff. The brigade headquarters building was even separate from the battalion headquarters building, where the line companies' offices were located.

But she was still wearing her ACUs. The unit patch on her shoulder, the vertical stripes and the dragon's head of the 89th MP Brigade, matched theirs. When she'd been given the all clear to exit the house by the dispatcher, she'd zipped up her jacket, put on her patrol cap and walked out with authority. Both MPs had snapped to attention and saluted, but she'd seen the surprise and question in their eyes, so she'd returned their salutes, tapped the unit patch on her shoulder and said, "Brigade S-3."

She wasn't going to jail today.

But this jerk in her driveway was completely blowing her secret about living with Tom. The two MPs on patrol were probably in the 410th, because that company was currently on rotation for garrison duty, but they would surely know who the commander of the 584th was. They probably saw Tom almost daily in the dining facility, around the offices, at the motor pool. If not, the computers in their patrol cars had already informed them that this house belonged to the commander of the 584th MP Company. The rumor mill was about to get very, very busy.

All thanks to this jerk, who'd scared her to death by rattling the sliding glass door and jiggling the kitchen window to see if it would open. She'd been barefoot, relaxing on the couch, when she'd heard those unmistakable sounds of forced entry. She'd honestly thought someone had seen the diamond ring on the windowsill and was trying to break in. Since she was an MP, she knew better than to go all Rambo and confront an intruder herself while she was barefoot in a brown T-shirt. That's what on-duty, armed MPs in bulletproof vests were for. It's what they loved, as a matter of fact. She'd rolled off the couch, scooped up her boots, run at a crouch into her bedroom and locked herself in—an instinctive move that took less than two seconds. She'd dialed 911 before it had been three seconds.

"I called 911," the jerk announced.

"Didn't we all?" she said sarcastically. She was all cool authority now, but for a few moments on her bedroom floor, her hands had shaken as she'd laced up her boots, her body pumping out adrenaline because there'd been the very real possibility that she was about to engage in unarmed close-quarters combat with an intruder.

A third patrol car came down the street, running with lights and sirens, because if there was one thing you did not screw with, it was another MP—or his house. Frankly, having three patrols respond was understated when the reported crime was at the house of an MP company commander. The watch commander was doing a good job restraining the rest of the patrols.

But all this attention wasn't good. This incident was going to be included in the police blotter. The blotter was a summary of the post's law enforcement activity that was delivered daily to Colonel Reed, who was the provost marshal of Fort Hood…and to the commander of III Corps, a three-star general.

Living in on-post housing had its disadvantages.

I'm sorry, Tom, but you're not going to be my dirty little secret much longer. She flushed at the thought. Dirty? Yes, they'd gotten down and dirty in the hallway this morning. But little? She'd had her palm on the *ceiling*. There was nothing little about Tom Cross. Nothing.

The third patrol car braked hard to stop. The passenger door opened, and Tom himself stepped out. Six foot two with every muscle ripped, Captain Tom Cross looked like he was going to kill someone.

Her knees went weak. *I slept with that.*

She saw his gaze go from her to the jerk and the jerk's car, to the two MPs, back to her—a fraction of a second. The MPs came to attention and saluted him. The jerk crossed his arms over his chest and said, "Well, well, well, it's about time—"

"You." Tom spat the word at the man, startling him. The man shut up.

Tom returned the MPs' salutes as he walked right up to her, *right* up to her, much too close. But he didn't touch her. "You're okay." He said it as a statement, but she knew he wanted to hear it from her.

"I'm okay."

He nodded once and turned around. "Report."

The corporal was the highest-ranking, so it fell on him to report to the furious captain. "Sir, we received a 911 call that an attempted burglary was in progress at this location. Shortly after that, we received another 911 call that there was an intruder in the house. It was unclear to us that these were two different callers. We thought the earlier attempted break-in had succeeded, and now there was an intruder in the house, but when I arrived on scene, this man claimed he'd made the call, and that he'd seen someone in the house. We covered the house with weapons drawn and gave the order for the intruder to come out. Captain Pallas was in the house, meanwhile, still on the line with dispatch, so we clarified that she was the alleged intruder. Weapons were holstered and then dispatch instructed her to exit the premises."

"She *is* the intruder." The jerk pulled out a military ID, offering it up between two fingers like he was deigning to let the MPs touch his card. "This is the home of an active duty soldier. Tom Cross is authorized to live here, and only Tom Cross. The US Army does not provide housing to girlfriends and other… recreational relationships. I do believe the army is still as strict on that principle as the air force is. She needs to go."

Helen was watching him closely, this arrogant man in the driveway, so she saw the way he was looking at Tom as he turned to him. His smile held contempt. "I do hope this doesn't hurt your record permanently."

"You idiot." Tom said it as a quiet rasp as he got in the man's face. "Weapons were drawn. You bet her life on the MPs' training and the dispatcher's ability to reach them by radio."

Helen believed, truly believed, Tom was going to strike the man. The moment was suspended in time as the two men faced off and then Helen saw the resemblance in their profiles, and her stomach lurched.

Tom grabbed the ID from the man and turned to hand it to the MPs. "Go ahead and write up what you need to. Captain Pallas is authorized to live here. Colonel Reed approved it. We'll be in the house."

"Reed?" the jerk said. "Oscar Reed? He's condoning cohabitation now, is he? In direct violation of regulations? We'll see what his superiors have to say about that."

"Get in the house." Tom waited until the man had taken a few steps toward the door, close enough for Helen to hear Tom speak quietly, with contempt in his own voice. "*Dad.* Get in the house with Mom. She is in the car."

Dad. The roiling in Helen's stomach stabilized into a knot.

"She's better off there. I'm in no mood for any more female hysterics."

"Go and get your wife out of the car. What is *wrong* with you?"

As his father—his father!—brushed past him to head for the car, Tom walked into the house. Helen stayed right beside him. The second they were inside, he shut the door and pulled her around to face him. He didn't let go of her arms. "Helen, I need you to be my wife."

"What? I am."

"I mean—don't tell them we're getting divorced. Don't— I don't want them to know about the blackout or Reed's orders or any of it."

"But why? These are your parents."

Tom suddenly grabbed her close, smashing her

against his chest. "Thank God, you're okay. I lost ten years off my life when that call came in. *Helen*." And he kissed her hair, her temple.

She'd hardly had a chance to process that emotional outburst when he let her go and answered her question. "Because my father will use you as a weapon— you, the memory of you, the fact that you were ever important to me. He'll twist it and make it ugly, and I don't want the son of a bitch to have the pleasure."

There was a fine tremor in his body now. She felt it in his hands on her arms. She'd felt it this morning, when she'd had all of him against the wall, all his attention, all his desire. His breath on her neck, that shout of surrender—passion.

His fingers tightened on her arms. "I'll give you what you want."

Sex? He was going to give her more sex?

"I'll divorce you in February."

Oh. Yes, of course. That was what she wanted.

The door behind him opened. He didn't look away from her, but silently mouthed one word, just as she'd done in Colonel Reed's office: *Please?*

She nodded, and he turned around to face his parents.

Her new in-laws.

Helen took Tom's hand in hers and held on tightly.

Chapter Twelve

"Hello, Mom."

"Hello, son."

Helen watched as Tom bent down to give his mother a brief kiss on her cheek. The perfectly coifed and contained woman reached up and patted his cheek, gently, twice. Then she tucked her hand back in her husband's arm like a debutante at a ball and stood there with a vacant smile on her face.

Wow. That was all the affection Tom got from his own mother? The woman didn't seem particularly cold or nasty, though. She smiled and looked very content.

Some families weren't demonstrative, Helen supposed. Since Tom's was not, it occurred to Helen to let go of Tom's hand, but his fingers were laced firmly with hers. Okay, then. They'd be the affectionate branch of the Cross family tree.

Today. Just for today.

Tom held her hand but faced his father squarely. "To what do I owe the pleasure of the ambush this time?"

"Your mother thought her only child should be visited for the holidays."

Tom spoke to his mother. "Then you could have invited me to Christmas dinner."

"Oh, goodness," she said with a little shake of her head. "Your father's schedule is so full."

"Today was the only time convenient." Brigadier General Cross set his sights on Helen. "However, I would not have agreed to come if I'd known my wife would be exposed to a woman her son saw fit to *entertain* in his home."

"Oh, goodness," Helen said drily.

Tom squeezed her hand and she glanced at him to see if that squeeze meant *behave*. These were Tom's parents. She needed to keep her snark to herself—even when she was faced with condescension from a couple who apparently thought they were living in a previous century.

But Tom was looking at her with something like approval. Pride?

"Before you get warmed up for a lecture about the sins of cohabitation, allow me to introduce Captain Helen Pallas, my wife. Helen, these are my parents, Alice and Norman Cross."

"It's General and Mrs. Norman Cross," his mother corrected gently.

"Wife?" General Cross asked. "*This* is what you meant when you said Reed had authorized this woman to live in your housing?"

Helen didn't like being referred to as *this*, but she

tried to channel her inner supportive wife and kept smiling politely. She could practically hear Russell scoffing in her brain. *You couldn't be a supportive wife if you tried.*

"What kind of marriage is this?"

"There's only one kind, Dad. Two people, commitment until death do you part."

Until Valentine's Day.

"But where is your ring, dear?" his mother asked.

That was Helen's cue to speak. "I left it by the kitchen sink."

Tom's parents just looked at her in silence. Had she said the wrong thing? Was she supposed to do something?

"Thank you for reminding me. I'd better go get it before I forget." She let go of Tom's hand and went into the kitchen. *I need you to be my wife*, he'd said, and now she understood what he'd meant. His parents were so…difficult. Judgmental. They thought it was outrageous that he was married. They'd put him through the wringer if he tried to explain that she had no memory of the wedding, or that she'd been ordered to live here until they could file for divorce. If Tom told them they'd met and married the same day, they would respond with scorn.

The thought made her heart hurt. Meeting and marrying the same day was crazy, but it was crazy-optimistic. Optimism didn't deserve scorn. No wonder Tom had asked her not to say anything. No wonder he'd been so desperate that he'd promised her February if she would pretend theirs wasn't a temporary arrangement.

February. That made her heart hurt, too. It was supposed to make her feel free.

The ring was where she'd left it, a little circle of perfection abandoned on a wooden windowsill. Helen picked it up and slid it on. It sparkled. Her breath caught—it was really something, to see a wedding ring on your finger for the first time when you knew it would be there forever. Wasn't it?

She felt a shiver down the back of her neck. Was that how she'd felt with this ring? Or was she remembering the first time she'd worn a ring, for Russell?

She returned to Tom's side and held out her hand cautiously. His parents wanted to see the ring, but she wasn't anticipating any joy in their reaction. More like an evaluation.

"Oh." His mother nodded as if *now* she could believe they were married.

"He shouldn't have bought you something that expensive if you don't know how to keep accountability of your belongings. Do you always leave valuables in the kitchen?"

General Cross had that scorn thing down cold. Helen smiled, though it killed her.

"Only when I'm cooking or cleaning." *Like a good little wife.* "I don't want to get margarine or something like that all gummed up in the setting." She looked at Tom, wanting to be convincing, but she was no actress. She had to stick to the truth. "Remember the margarine? I wouldn't want to go through all that again."

He picked up her hand and smoothed his thumb over the diamonds. "No harm done. It's as good as new." Then he linked his fingers with hers once more.

She placed her other hand over his and leaned her

whole body into him. It felt odd to demonstrate physical affection in uniform, but they were in his house, so it was allowed. Besides, she wanted the support. Or she wanted him to have the support.

The general utterly dismissed her with a disgusted glance at their hands, then he focused his ire on Tom. "So that's it. You're married. You decided not to request my approval, because Oscar Reed condoned it, didn't you? It wasn't enough that he turned you away from flying and sucked you into the army, now he's taken it upon himself to make decisions that belong to your family. He knew about the marriage before your own parents knew."

"He's the brigade commander. Helen and I are in the same brigade. He knows. As for the rest, I won't rehash your expectations for me. I told you I was done with that when I was eighteen, and that has not changed."

Oscar Reed? Oscar? Tom's family had a history with the brigade commander that Helen hadn't guessed at. She hoped her surprise and curiosity didn't show. Her polite expression was, perhaps, not as vacant as Alice's, but it was as close as she could approximate.

"The only thing that has changed is that you now have a daughter-in-law," Tom said.

Helen tried to be sweet and supportive, and smooth things over for her husband. "It's a pleasure to meet you both."

His father and mother stared at her in silence, one hostilely, one vacantly.

To heck with it. She could only be herself, and she had questions. *Jeez, Helen, can't just sit there and shut up for five minutes, can you?*

She shoved Russell's voice out of her head. "It's

particularly pleasant to meet you now that I know you aren't trying to break into the house. Why *were* you trying to open the sliding glass door?"

Neither parent answered her. The silence was chilly.

"He was hoping to get in my house before I got home." Tom sighed. "Still think you have the right to conduct pop inspections, Dad? You miss the glory days, back when you treated your family the way you treated your flight crews."

His father apparently found it more convenient to ignore Tom's statement and answer Helen's question instead. "This is our son's house. It's perfectly acceptable for his parents to make themselves at home. I have every right to look for an unlocked door or a hidden key."

Tom stepped in front of her, so she only saw his broad back instead of his father's hateful face. Hateful wasn't too strong of a word. Arrogant. Selfish. They all fit.

"This is my wife's house," Tom said, "and you were attempting to break in. If you ever pull this crap again, I will charge you with trespassing. Are we clear?"

More silence.

I would at least try *to be a decent father,* Tom had said, as they'd watched an awful wedding movie and talked about regrets. She understood now where he'd been coming from. His childhood must have been warped by his father's dysfunctions. But if Tom ever had a child, he was determined not to pass on that hurt. She didn't know how a person could find the strength to break out of a mold that had been forced upon him since birth, but Tom had done it.

She stepped from behind him to stand at his side,

taking his hand in hers. General Cross was refusing to respond, standing like a statue, looking at Tom but not really looking at him. Tom had done that in the dark kitchen that first night, when she'd taken off her ring. But Tom had caught himself doing it. He'd apologized. He'd given her room. He'd broken the mold.

His father was still stuck.

"You don't want to talk to me, Dad? That's okay. I don't want to talk to you." Tom let go of Helen's hand and moved to open the door.

"You were not dismissed," the general said.

Tom turned back to his father. "That doesn't count as conversation between a father and a son. I'll remind you again, you are not a hotshot pilot, and I am not a boy. It's time to move on. We can't have any kind of relationship until you do."

"Oh, goodness," Alice said.

Tom shook his head at his mother. Helen saw the resignation in his eyes. "If you'll excuse me, there are three patrol cars outside my house right now, waiting for my orders."

"Patrol cars," his father scoffed. "You could have been a fighter pilot."

Resignation was obliterated by a flash of disgust. "You should be very glad I chose not to become a pilot, because right now, I am the only chance you have to avoid being charged for intentionally placing a false 911 call. This isn't your turf. Remember that, the next time you feel the need to thump your chest and pick a fight to see if you're still the king of the jungle. You aren't."

Helen watched him put on his patrol cap, pull the brim low and walk out into the December sun. She turned to her new father-in-law. "He's right. You aren't it. He is."

Then she put on her own patrol cap and walked out the door, too.

Tom took Helen's ID and his father's ID from the corporal's outstretched hand. He could practically feel the man's relief to be done with them and gone from the scene.

"Merry Christmas, sir."

"You, too."

Undoubtedly, Dad would convince himself that he'd gotten away without punishment because he was too intimidating for a corporal to dare to arrest him, but that was a delusion. It wasn't that an MP was reluctant to arrest a retired air force officer; it was that no MP wanted to arrest the father of Captain Cross. That was not because they were intimidated by Tom. They respected him. Tom took care of his troops. They took care of him.

He sure as hell hadn't learned that kind of leadership from his father.

But he had learned it, and that was what mattered. Professionally, Tom was no longer either rebelling against his father or trying to impress him. He wasn't out to meet anyone's standards but his own, and his own were pretty damned high, thanks to the examples set for him over the years by good leaders like Colonel Reed.

Tom watched the three patrol cars take off. He'd been satisfied with his career for some time now. Hadn't he told Helen so at that first marriage counseling appointment? He hadn't wanted fame because it would only get in the way of his service. But it wasn't until today that he consciously realized his father's negativity no longer had any influence in his professional life. He'd been free of that for years.

Tom looked at the IDs in his hand, his father's and Helen's. He couldn't say the same of his personal life.

Those walls around his heart had originally been a defense against his father's calculated emotional abuse. It wasn't until Las Vegas, it wasn't until Helen Pallas, that Tom had first realized how long he'd left those walls in place without question. He'd been allowing his father's negative influence to prevent him from loving someone who could love him back.

Until Helen.

He'd wanted Helen more than he'd wanted to stay behind a wall, but then the unthinkable had happened, and, once more, Tom had been left loving someone who didn't love him back. He'd spent every moment since then doing exactly what his father had taught him to do: putting the walls back up. Trying to build them higher.

It wasn't working.

He tapped the ID cards on his hand. The way he'd felt when the 911 call had come in made it undeniable: Tom loved Helen. It didn't matter what she remembered. It didn't matter whether or not she ever loved him back. He loved her.

I feel awful... I don't mean to disappoint you over and over... It's tearing me up to live like this.

He loved her, even if that meant letting her go.

He turned around, and there she was, smiling at him in the cool December sun. He didn't try to put up a wall; his heart just took the stab of pain.

"The MPs left?" she asked, although it wasn't really a question. "No arrests?"

"Not this time."

She stepped closer and tilted her head, looking up at him from under her brim. "I thought you said your childhood was like mine?"

He touched her cheek with the back of his hand, a brief caress of the face he loved. "Mom fed me three meals a day. Dad never broke my arm."

"Oh, Tom." He saw the shine of unshed tears in her eyes. She may not remember loving him, but she was softhearted enough to care for the boy he'd once been. "What's next?"

"Let's go get rid of my father." He put his arm around her shoulders as they walked toward the house together, touching her while he still could.

Chapter Thirteen

Helen had never been so excited to boil water in her life.

They were going to eat dinner together.

She'd said it so casually, after his parents had driven away. "I'm starving. If I make spaghetti, would you help me eat it?"

He'd barely paused. "Sounds good. Thanks."

He'd gone into his bedroom, so she'd gone into hers. Baggy camouflage had been dumped in favor of skin-tight but stretchy black yoga pants and a pink, low-cut top that was too clingy for her to wear any place she might run into the soldiers she worked with. Not too clingy to stay at home with a man who'd already carried her into a shower, naked and sated.

She set two place settings on the table, directly across from each other, because she wanted that blue gaze on her once more. When he'd looked at her after his parents had left, he'd looked a little sad. She wanted him to look at her the way he had this morning. The way he had at that casino. She tugged down her pink top.

Come find me.

She walked back into the kitchen. He was standing there, his back to her, staring at the pot of hot water. God's reason for blue jeans. She'd wrapped her legs around his waist this morning. She'd held his hand and stood by his side this afternoon. She looked at him now, and felt shy.

"Hi," she said.

He looked up, and she felt that little jolt when their eyes met. His gaze dropped down to her hips, rose to linger on her cleavage for a heart-stopping second, returned to her eyes. In half a step, he reached her and picked up her hand, then carried it to his lips. "You were amazing today."

"Oh." She watched his lips kiss her hand, and remembered them hot on nylon panties, her hand pressed to the ceiling. "So were you."

He hesitated, then held her gaze as he spoke over the back of her hand. "You were amazing with my parents. Thank you."

She'd sounded so breathy. He sounded very deliberate as he clarified what had been so amazing. His mind wasn't where hers was. Shyness turned to mortification.

She forced herself to say something. "I can see why you wouldn't want them to know your personal details."

More and more serious—she was killing the mood

she'd wanted to set with her dinner and her pink top. "I'm sorry."

He looked at her hand, not at her. With his other hand, he touched the diamond circlet, then held it between his finger and thumb, and gave it a little twist. It slid right off, but Helen made a little gasp of pain. "I thought you said you would never take that ring off me."

He set it on the windowsill. "I also said I would never divorce you. I promised you this afternoon I would."

She hadn't been thinking of this afternoon. This morning, two bodies, one intent, one pleasure... He'd promised to divorce her. "But not until February."

He misunderstood the disappointment in her voice. "That's as soon as I can, legally. Colonel Reed wants to see us in his office tomorrow morning—"

"On Saturday? Why?" This was confusing. It was all confusing.

"My guess is that he got a preview of the police blotter from the watch commander."

"Oh, yes. That." She'd been scared. Called 911.

Tom gave her fingers a squeeze and dropped her hand. "While we're there, we can tell him we've come to an agreement. Maybe now that we've gone to a few marriage counseling appointments, he'll let you move out sooner. I can't make the divorce happen faster than February, but I'm willing to try to get you some relief."

Relief? He didn't want to know what kind of relief she was aching for. She wanted more of what they'd had this morning. He wanted her to move out.

"I've had time to think about it," he said. "When

you told me in Jennifer's office that dragging this out was a punishment for you, I should have listened."

You had sex with me, and now you've decided I can go.

She pressed her ring-free hand against her stomach, but the nausea still turned into a knot. Russell's taunts, his accusations, gurgled up. *Just once, you could be late to formation. You're too tired for anything but the basics. Very basic.* The insecurity overwhelmed her. She was bad in bed. That's why Russell had been unfaithful. That's why Tom no longer cared if she wore her ring.

She turned on her heel and stepped out of the kitchen.

"Helen?"

The hallway lay just to her right. This morning had been… She'd actually been late to formation. She hadn't rushed, not when her lover had put her in a steamy shower and left her feeling so deliciously languid. That plain, white wall? That had been anything but basic. That had been— Russell had probably never imagined that position.

Tom was right behind her. "Helen, I didn't mean to—"

"We should talk about this morning." She sounded like a robot, monotone. Monotonous. What an invitation to sex.

Tom was silent, but she waited. After this afternoon, she knew he hated silence for an answer as much as she did. His father was even worse than Russell. Tom was just thinking of the right words to say.

He said them. "This morning was good, but it probably wasn't a good idea."

She died inside.

"We're supposed to be building emotional intimacy. Friendship. The romantic intimacy is… Those memories are gone."

Maybe not. I first saw you in a casino. But that would sound too desperate, too much like begging. *Wait, give me a chance, I remembered one thing. I remembered thirty seconds out of fourteen hours.*

"Sexual intimacy was not on the agenda," he said, sounding clinical. "I don't really want to discuss it with Jennifer, either, so we shouldn't—"

"This morning will be our dirty little secret."

That shut him up. Whether it was the actual words or just the sarcasm in her voice, it shut him up.

"The timing here sucks," she said. "My household goods are due to arrive tomorrow, sometime between noon and four. Even if Colonel Reed agrees to let me find my own place tomorrow morning, I don't think I can sign a lease and redirect a moving van before noon."

"No." He ran a hand down her arm, a soothing gesture. "But we'll work it out. If you leave everything in boxes, it won't be too hard to move when you get your own place."

She didn't want to be soothed. She shook off his hand and went back to the stove. The water had started to boil. "There's furniture, too. It's not going to all fit in the spare bedroom."

"I'll be here tomorrow. We'll work on it together. It'll give us something to talk about with Jennifer. She'll be happy we worked as a team."

Yes, Jennifer would be happy. *But not me.*

Helen dumped the spaghetti in the water and set the timer. "Your supper will be ready in eight minutes."

She headed for the front door, grabbing her coat and her car keys on the way.

"Where are you going?" Tom asked, as if it was amazing she wouldn't want to stay and eat spaghetti with him after he'd told her sex was a mistake and he'd help her move out.

"It's Friday night. I'm going to the pub."

Tom shoveled spaghetti into his mouth as he stood at the kitchen sink, glaring at the diamond ring.

His car was still at the headquarters building. He'd come home in an MP cruiser going sixty in a thirty, running with lights and sirens. He could call the station on a back line, ask them to send a patrol car around if things were slow, get a ride to the Legends Pub. Hypothetically, he could do that. It would probably be a small abuse of power. It would be a huge chunk of grist for the rumor mill. Things were already going to be bad enough with his frigging father calling 911 to report that Captain Pallas was in Captain Cross's house.

What a nightmare of a day. Except for the morning, up against the wall. The fact that he'd just killed all possibility of ever having another morning like that made a drink sound all the more necessary. Helen had beaten him to it, though, leaving for the pub and leaving him high and dry at home without a vehicle.

She won't be drinking cranberry juice this time.

He wouldn't, either, if he were in her place. He shoveled in another forkful of spaghetti, then he nearly choked on it. Helen. Drinking. She had no drink tolerance. She could black out again, and he'd made a vow. *Every single week that I'm with you, I'm going to make sure that someone I cherish doesn't black out anywhere unsafe or with anyone who might be unsafe.*

It wasn't February yet. He was with her this week.

He pulled out his phone and called the station. Colonel Reed was going to have a field day with him tomorrow, but Tom was going to take care of Helen tonight.

"Oops. Sorry. That seat is taken. My boyfriend's going to be here in just a few minutes."

Tom shook his head as he spied on Helen. She was sitting alone at a little table for two. She'd used that line twice already in the five minutes he'd been here, and the place was half-empty. It was Friday night, but Christmas was on Tuesday, so half the men of Fort Hood were out of town on leave. The other half…

"Oops. Sorry. My boyfriend is using that chair."

The bored-looking cocktail waitress brought Helen a highball glass of something golden brown over ice. That wasn't a single shot of cola on the rocks. His bride was drinking scotch—and every man in the place was keeping one eye on the woman in the low-cut pink top as she did.

Tom walked over and pulled out the empty chair.

"Oops. Sorry. My boyfriend…"

"Has arrived."

"Tom."

"Yes."

"You are not my boyfriend." She toasted him with her glass. "You're my husband. You were never my boyfriend."

"I was for about fourteen hours."

She wagged one finger at him. "Nope. I don't remember that. I just woke up with a husband. Bam. That's kind of a lot to deal with first thing in the morning, don't you think?"

It was. He hadn't thought of it that way. He'd been so hurt she hadn't stayed and listened to him, hadn't stayed and tried to be a wife to a total stranger…damn. The last of that resentment he'd harbored against her for *not even trying* fizzled out.

"But you are indeed my husband, aren't you? All the way until Valentine's Day." She tilted her head back and downed her drink. She used the glass to point at him. "*Through* Valentine's Day. What are you going to get your wife for Valentine's Day? I deserve chocolate before you divorce me. It better be a giant box of chocolate."

"How many drinks have we had tonight?"

"We? I don't know. How many have you had?"

"Zero."

"Excellent." She dug in her jacket pocket for her keys and slapped them on the table. "Here you go. Let's see. Zero plus three makes three. *We* have had three drinks."

"Impressive." She hadn't been here more than an hour. Three scotches in an hour? She hadn't had that much in the fourteen hours before they'd married. They'd only had one drink after the wedding, on the house in the high roller room as they'd waited for the honeymoon suite to be ready. They'd waited impatiently, unimpressed by the gamblers who'd been betting ten thousand minimums per hand at the blackjack table. They'd had more exciting things to look at: each other.

But she didn't remember that. At triple that drink

rate, she wasn't going to remember a thing tonight, either. With any luck, she'd forget meeting her miserable new in-laws this afternoon, too. It was a sure thing, however, that she had to be standing with him at Colonel Reed's desk tomorrow morning.

He stood and offered her his hand. "Come on, Cinderella. Let me get you home before midnight."

"Have a seat, both of you."

Helen sat next to Tom. She only felt slightly green around the gills. A glass of water would be nice, though. Scotch always made her thirsty the morning after.

Tom kept giving her the strangest looks. He'd asked her how she felt at least three times. He'd asked her what time she'd left for the pub, how she'd gotten home—questions he knew the answers to. *You drove me home, and don't ask me that again. It's getting annoying.*

Colonel Reed looked between the two of them. "I don't have to tell you why I've called you two in, do I?"

Tom was silent.

Helen took a stab at it. "Sir, it could be any of a variety of things. It's been quite the month."

"Wise guy, are you?"

"No, sir." But she was being one. She had a terrible feeling in her chest and sitting next to Tom was only making it worse. She had lost him. He didn't want to continue working on their emotional intimacy, and he'd stone-cold turned her down for any sexual intimacy. He'd sworn he would never take off her ring, that he would never divorce her, and he'd changed his mind about both.

She'd warned him. From the first morning in Vegas, she'd warned him that he'd be better off without her as a wife. There was something about her that made men unhappy to live with her, as he was proving once again.

She could do nothing about it. She couldn't make her brain produce the memories Tom so desperately wanted, and he didn't want her without them. Oh, yeah—and today, Russell's damned furniture was going to arrive.

Tiptoeing close to that line of insubordination with Colonel Reed on a Saturday morning hardly seemed to matter. It should—her career was all she'd have left shortly—but it didn't.

Tom took a stab at it, a better stab than she had. "Sir, I assume our names appeared on the police blotter this morning. Captain Pallas could not have done anything differently. It would have been foolish of her not to call 911 in the circumstances. She has no experience with General Cross and his ambushes. It's on me. I should have predicted he was due for a little check-in with his son."

"Tom. You aren't responsible for your father's behavior. You never were."

Helen frowned. There it was again, that implication that Colonel Reed and the Cross family went way back. "May I ask a question, sir?"

"Shoot."

Tom says that, too. He behaved more like Colonel Reed than his father.

She turned to Tom. "I should ask you this question. On the day I arrived, you had already told the brigade commander about Vegas, but you are a company commander. You report to the *battalion* commander. Why didn't you tell your battalion commander? Why did you skip to my commander?"

"I've known Colonel Reed since I was nine. I didn't know you were going to be in the brigade. I'd come in to talk to him because I...trust his advice. Usually. Until he forced you to live in my house."

She wasn't prepared for the insult. She gasped.

Tom lunged forward in his chair and put his hand on her thigh. "I didn't mean it like that. That's not an insult to you. I meant he had no right to make your life difficult and to deny you the right to live where you liked."

She couldn't doubt the sincerity on his face. She nodded, but she didn't trust her voice.

Tom looked at Colonel Reed. "And it's unfortunate that her name got dragged onto the police blotter today, because that will also make her life difficult, and it is also not her fault."

Colonel Reed raised an eyebrow and looked pointedly at Tom's hand on her thigh. She hadn't really noticed it until then. Tom touched her a lot, especially when they were seated close like this at the counselor's office.

Colonel Reed waited until Tom removed his hand before speaking again. "I'm letting your insult to my judgment about housing arrangements slide for the moment. Neither one of you are on the police blotter today. Between you, me and the watch commander, this meeting is a behind-chewing of epic proportions and a punishment far worse than having your names on a blotter, stoking the rumor mill. When you leave, try to look duly chastened and abject."

Helen almost laughed in relief. "Yes, sir."

"Go. Leave. And Merry Christmas."

"Yes, sir." She got up with alacrity. There was a water fountain in the hallway, and those scotches had not been kind.

"Before we go, sir, there's something I need to discuss with you and Captain Pallas."

Helen slowly sat down again. Couldn't Tom save it for another day?

"On the day that she arrived, I told you she'd drunk to excess and blacked out. I didn't say it that bluntly, but it is what I said. It was what I believed to be true, despite her claims to the contrary. I gave you cause to doubt her character before she'd had a chance to make a first impression, sir. Helen, I'm sorry."

"What prompted this little moment of awareness?" the colonel asked.

"We went to the pub last night. She drank more than she did in Vegas, and as you can see, she's hardly worse for wear. She told us she'd never had a problem drinking before, and I should have believed her."

"I gave her the benefit of the doubt, Tom. It was you that I worried about. What kind of man would stand by and watch his bride get so inebriated that it was dangerous? I thought I raised you better than that."

Helen would have been charmed at this big-brother relationship if she weren't so offended that it had taken Tom this long to believe her. She'd had to drink last night to prove she didn't drink. Or something like that.

"Here's the real question," she said. "Alcohol didn't make me black out. What did?"

"You asked the counselor about that. Poor sleep. High stress."

Helen waved that away. "Please. I've been in the

army how many years? If no sleep and high stress made me lose whole days of memory, I'd still think I was a new second lieutenant."

Colonel Reed laughed at that one. She was glad someone was amused.

"I must have been drugged," she said quietly. "Think about it. A drug like roofies would do it."

Nobody was amused.

"Roofies." The word exploded into the room. "The date rape drug. You think I would roofie my own bride? That I would roofie any woman, any woman on the planet?"

"No, I didn't mean—"

"Even if I was that depraved, I wouldn't have needed roofies with you." Tom stood. "Think about it, Helen. God, just yesterday— Why would roofies ever be— Do you really think roofies would *ever* be necessary—"

"I didn't mean you drugged me. But someone did."

"We had a bed of roses. Why in the hell would I arrange a bed of roses if I was just going to drug you unconscious?"

"Tom. Stop." She bit her lip and turned to the colonel. "I'm sorry, sir. TMI. You didn't need to know that."

The colonel waved it off. "I'm going to assume that came standard with a honeymoon suite. Tom, she has a valid point here."

Tom had assumed the position *at ease*, feet apart, hands clasped behind his back, but there was nothing relaxed about it. He was keeping himself from pacing in fury in the commander's office. "It wasn't roofies.

That would have knocked her out. We were…awake until dawn."

"Ecstasy, then. Maybe cocaine." The colonel looked at her sharply. "Were you given a urine test for drug screening as part of in-processing?"

"No, sir."

"Good. Write a letter stating the date you suspect you were drugged and the symptoms. I want it on my desk the day after Christmas. I'll witness it and date it, and I will keep it on file for the next thirty days. If you get pulled for a random drug screen in that time and it does come up positive for who-knows-what, you'll need that documentation. If you aren't tested, I'll destroy the document."

"Thank you, sir." Helen felt all her good fortune to be working for a man who took care of his personnel so well. She glanced at Tom. Or perhaps he was looking out for his younger brother's bride.

As she looked at him, Tom's color suddenly paled. "Absinthe."

Helen felt a taste of remembered licorice, a green liqueur that swirled as it turned cloudy.

Tom sat down heavily. "Helen, you drank absinthe after the ceremony. Back at the hotel."

The colonel shrugged. "Modern absinthe is just a liqueur. It's illegal to sell the original absinthe, the kind that got everyone addicted and made them see green fairies. Since it's been outlawed, I would bet real absinthe would cost hundreds of dollars a glass, like a designer street drug."

"It did cost hundreds. We're talking about Vegas. If someone pays a hundred dollars for an alcoholic beverage that's supposed to give them a legendary kick, the bar probably adds a little boost to make sure they get their money's worth."

"Yes," Colonel Reed said, "that sounds likely."

Helen could feel the colonel looking at her, but she couldn't take her eyes off Tom. She didn't know what to say to him. His wife would know, but she did not. She could barely swallow, her mouth was so dry.

Tom scrubbed his face with his hands and broke the brief silence. "The high roller room. VIP. Those people were betting ten grand a hand. Cocaine, ecstasy. You think those were available for the right price?" He laughed without mirth. "Of course they were."

He bent forward under the weight of it, forearms resting on his legs like he'd just carried a hundred-pound rucksack for a hundred miles. "I'm sorry, Helen. They put us in the high roller room and offered us a drink on the house while they were setting up the penthouse suite to my specifications. I had a century-old single malt. You had absinthe. You liked the crystal glass it came in. An antique, with gold accessories for the sugar cube and the water."

Then he'd made sure his wife was given a crystal glass for her orange juice the next morning, because he knew she liked crystal.

Oh, Tom...you loved her.

She couldn't speak. She couldn't swallow.

"They needed time to set up the rose petals." Tom laughed again, a terrible sound. "If I hadn't ordered rose petals, I would still have my wife."

He missed her terribly. Grieved her absence. Helen wished that woman still existed, too.

"I'm sorry," she whispered, one more time. "I don't remember."

Chapter Fourteen

*F*ragile.

The word meant nothing. Every moving box she'd labeled *Fragile* had been haphazardly tossed off the moving van to form a sloppy pile in Tom's garage. She and Tom had been in the spare bedroom, so they hadn't seen it happening. Instead, they'd been disassembling the futon couch to make room for her queen-size bed. That bed. The one she'd shared with Russell, and he'd shared with other women.

It was just a bed, and she'd be glad to have a real mattress instead of a futon.

Tom kept looking at her with hungry eyes, because she looked like the woman he'd loved and lost. She felt the weight of it and escaped to the garage to turn the boxes right side up.

Then a car pulled up to the curb and parked behind

the moving van, and her world turned sideways again. Russell Gannon got out of the car, and the smug look on his face sent her back in time. She was nothing, a poor excuse for a wife, lousy in bed, unwanted.

She turned around, ready to run into the house, but the door opened and Tom walked out. Now he would see the real her. She was not this paragon of a woman he'd married one night in Vegas. Russell would expose her for the mess she was, and he'd enjoy every minute of it.

She grabbed Tom by the arms. "I need you to be my husband. Please. That's my ex, coming up the curb. Don't tell him we're leaving the boxes packed until I move out. He'll—he'll laugh at me. I'll give you what you want, Tom. I'll wait until June, and I'll do the filing. Please?"

Tom glanced over her head, but she wouldn't turn around to watch Russell walking up Tom's driveway. It just seemed so wrong for Russell to be here, like a bad dream where she had to take a test, but she had to write with a dead fish instead of a fountain pen.

She felt Tom's biceps flex under her fingers as he raised his hands to cup her face. She clung to him, fingers digging in, although his kiss was gentle. Soothing. Then he licked her lower lip, and she opened her mouth, and the kiss went deep, fast and hard. They kissed like they were in the hallway—or like they were surrounded by gold and crystal and she couldn't think of a reason to stop kissing him, because he was so sexy and she was safe with him, so she might as well pull him down with her to the hotel suite's couch and push that towel out of the way.

Tom finished the kiss, but she needed to cling to

him for balance for just another little moment. He looked over her head again, and this time, he smiled a kind of arrogant smile. She turned her head, and there was Russell, looking uncertain instead of smug as he stood just outside the open garage door. "H-Helen?"

She let go of Tom and turned all the way around, but Tom wrapped his arms around her from behind and kept her snug against his chest.

Russell recovered a bit. She recognized the set of his jaw. He was about to tell her what to do. "I just got here a couple of days ago and set up my new place. I went to the trouble of finding out where and when your household goods were being delivered, because I'm going to need a few things, after all."

"We're divorced, Russell. We settled all the property."

He smirked a bit at that. "It takes paperwork a while to catch up in the army. You know that. How easy do you think it was for me to call and find out about the household goods from Gannon in Seattle?" He nodded toward the pile of boxes. "You're going to need to open these now. You can't let them sit there for a month like you did last move. I want that giant spaghetti pot back. I'm going to need the silverware, too."

Tom laughed, a deep sound she felt in his chest as she stayed securely in his arms. "You're divorced, Russell. You are divorced and I am married, and you aren't touching anything that belongs to my wife." He let one hand drift slowly across her stomach to rest on her hip. "Anything."

Russell seemed mesmerized by her body for a moment, then his eyebrows snapped together. "Wait a minute. Married?"

"Yes," she said, with a sigh. She snuggled back into Tom a bit, who was making her feel like she was his bombshell of a trophy wife. She felt sexier with him because she was sexier with him. Russell was no Tom Cross. A sexier man made her a sexier woman. She should have known.

Russell seemed offended at her marriage. "We've only been divorced for, like, three weeks. Three weeks. How could you get married again so fast?"

She smiled at him like she was the cat who'd gotten the cream. "Vegas, baby."

In a few minutes, it was over. Russell had spluttered a little bit more and made one attempt to touch a box marked *Fragile*, and Tom had put an end to that by walking up to him and asking one, quiet question: *What part of the term* anything *don't you comprehend?*

Russell drove away empty-handed, without Helen's silverware or her spaghetti pot, and without even the tiniest piece of her heart.

She knew she was smiling like a kid at Christmas when she turned to Tom. "That was great. You were great. Did you see his face? Finally, I feel like I am well and truly done with that man. Divorced, with a capital D. Thank you."

"You're welcome." Tom's smile was only pleasant. Friendly. He pushed a length of her hair back, but only because it had fallen in her eyes. He didn't tug on it playfully, he didn't use it to hold her in place so he could kiss her neck, and he didn't smooth it back and cup her head and ask her if she remembered. "You didn't need to beg me to handle Russell. Don't worry about the deal for June. I'll still file in February."

Her fragile heart cracked into a thousand pieces as he picked up a box and stacked it neatly away.

He thought, for a moment, that Helen was laughing.

He stood in the dark hallway outside the door to the spare bedroom and listened.

She was crying.

He should let her have her privacy. It was nearly midnight, and she probably thought he was asleep, and they were married on paper only, so it really wasn't his place to sit beside her on a bed and chase away whatever she feared in the dark.

But it was Christmas. It had been a barren Christmas, spent doing trivial paperwork in their offices. She had volunteered to be the brigade duty officer. He had volunteered to be the battalion duty officer. Their offices were not in the same building.

It wasn't midnight yet. He couldn't let her cry alone on Christmas Day. He turned the knob and opened the door. "Hey, Helen. What's going on?"

"Oh." He'd startled her. In the dark, he heard a little scurry of movement. He could see enough to know she was standing at the foot of the bed, clutching a pillow to her chest. "It's nothing."

"Right."

She didn't seem inclined to say anything else, but then again, he hadn't asked her to. If he asked her a question, she would answer, because she was still the same woman he'd married, and Helen would never give him the silent treatment, not for as long as they both lived.

"What's making you cry, Helen?"

She took a long time to answer him, but she did answer him with a sigh. "Memories."

"The lack of them?" God knew that made him want to cry, too.

But she laughed a little with a hitch in her breath. "There are some I do remember that I'd like to forget. This bed—I thought it would be okay. I really have no love in my heart for Russell, so I thought this bed would be okay, but I can't get that memory out of my head."

Aw, hell. This was the actual bed she'd caught her husband screwing another woman on.

"And I feel like such a fool. It's an inanimate object. What's the big deal? But it's been hard these past couple nights. Then I thought, well, I'll just sleep on his side of the bed instead of the side where he—where I remember seeing him. But I have to tell you, Tom, and I know you'll laugh at me, but I want to assemble that futon sofa again and use that instead."

"I'm not laughing."

And then she was crying again, and he couldn't stand there and do nothing. *Love-honor-cherish.*

That pillow she clutched, for starters, wasn't good enough for her. He tossed the pillow on the bed and pulled her into his chest. She could cry there instead.

"I'm not crying over him."

"No? My shirt sure is getting wet while you're not crying over him." He said it kindly. He wanted to lighten up the night a bit, but it was hard for him to speak with any equanimity at all. He was jealous of Russell, jealous that she was shedding a single tear over that marriage. It ate him up inside, that her divorce with Russell made her sad, but her divorce with him couldn't happen soon enough to make her happy.

"That bed is just a kind of brutal reminder that my life is not going to be the way I'd envisioned it. I never thought I'd be such a bad partner. But I must have been, because Russell divorced me. And I have been the biggest disappointment of all to you, because now you're divorcing me, too."

"Helen, you *asked* me to divorce you."

"Because I knew I was going to disappoint you. And I did."

"I'm not disappointed in you." But as soon as he said it, he knew she'd never been blind.

"Tom." She took a shaky breath. "The fact that I don't remember is the biggest disappointment of your life. That's why February is okay with you now."

He rested his cheek against her and rocked with her a little bit in the dark. "February terrifies me."

The words had come out as he thought them, but they were true, and they needed to be said. "I'm letting you go because you said being married to me without your memories causes you pain. I don't want to cause you pain. But I'm afraid if your memory does come back and we're divorced, you'll never forgive me. I can imagine you saying, 'How could you, Tom? How could you let me go?'"

"Oh, Tom. She sounds very devoted to you, that Helen you know. I can't bring her back. I can't be her."

"You don't have to stop being who you are and become someone else. You're Helen. I promised I would love you forever, and that won't change."

She took in a shivery breath. "That's…that's kind of scary for me."

He scared her?

"The thing is, I can completely believe that I fell in love with you and jumped at the chance to marry you. You are…" She pulled away from him a little bit and flapped a hand to indicate his whole body. "You are exactly my cup of tea. I mean, you are ridiculously attractive. Lizzy and Michelle weren't the only ones lusting over you at the pub. I was practically drooling, but it kind of makes me sad, because if we'd met at the pub, we'd be dating and falling in love together at the same time."

We did fall in love at the same time. He'd told her that before. It hadn't helped. Maybe he should stop pushing her to fast-forward. Maybe he should just listen.

"Instead, it's like we're at two different places on a timeline." She stepped back and held her hands far apart. "You're all the way over here, at the finish line. You already crossed it and married me. But I'm way back here, at the beginning." She looked between her hands, and then she looked up at him, and he thanked God there was enough starlight coming through the window that he could see her wink. He'd treasure the memory of that wink.

She brought her hands closer together. A lot closer together. "Maybe it's more like this. I can see the finish line. If we'd started out at the same place, I would definitely be hoping you were going to pop the question. I can imagine being married to you in a way I've never been able to imagine it with anyone else."

Because we already are married, he wanted to say, but for once, silence might be the best response. He settled for a smile.

"But that future already happened. I wore the white dress and made the vows. It's like I'm in a terrible time warp, with everything happening out of order."

"You told me that over a glass of scotch, just a few nights ago. You woke up with a husband, you said."

"Bam."

"It was crazy for me to expect you to stay that morning in Las Vegas. If I woke up with a woman who told me she was my wife and I should blow off army orders to stay with her, I'd run out the door with a croissant in my hand, too. More bacon than you took, though." He pushed her hair back from her face. Her tears were drying.

"You're not still mad at me for that?"

"Nope. I have a question to ask you, and it might sound crazy, considering all the things you *do* remember. You've already survived your in-laws and we've already had some fights, issues at work, three sessions of marriage counseling and at least two rounds of sex that were better than any two other people have ever had."

He saw the flash of her white smile in the dark room, and it gave him hope.

"But despite all the memories we already share, I'd like to get to know you better. Helen Pallas, I think you are very pretty and a little bit of a smart-mouth and a very sharp officer. Can I take you on a date?"

"A date?"

"Well, yeah. If I married a girl at one-thirty on a Sunday morning and three weeks later wanted to get to know her better, I'd probably ask her if she wanted to get coffee or something. Maybe go to a party that weekend. Maybe I could take you to a movie. I'm pretty sure I can scrape together the money. That ROTC scholarship has paid off."

"Oh, Tom." Helen was crying—no, this time, she was laughing. "I think all the coffee shops and movie theaters are closed right now. But maybe we could get a blanket and lie on it and look at the stars. I would love to do that with you."

"It's December twenty-fifth. It's freezing cold out there." He scooped her up in his arms like she was as light as a feather, because to a guy like him, she was. "But I do know where there's a blanket we can lie on."

"I'm so glad I'm going to be dating you." She tucked her head into the space between his shoulder and his neck as he carried her down the hall.

He laid her on his bed. "Here is a blanket. We can talk all night. No pressure. We're on our own crazy schedule, and we don't have to do a damned thing we don't want to do in February or June or any other day of the year."

They did talk, but that led to more of the best sex any two people ever had and then they fell asleep together. When Tom's alarm went off, very early, he had to go to work and lead PT, because he was the company commander and had to set the example. He kissed her on the cheek as he left.

Helen smiled because she wasn't awake enough to laugh, then she slipped back into sleep and had a lovely dream. She dreamed about a glass elevator, about a blue-eyed man who'd found her on the fifth floor by an ice cream parlor where he'd licked whipped cream off his fingers. She dreamed about sitting by a resort pool, looking at his bare feet next to her bare feet, loving the way he touched her by sliding his ankle between hers as they ate lunch at a little table. She dreamed about all the wedding gowns she didn't buy and about the one she did, and her breath caught in her sleep when she stood in the jewelry store with Tom and he slid that diamond band on her hand for the first time, and she knew she would wear it forever. And she dreamed about the high roller lounge, how she and Tom had sipped ridiculously expensive drinks and scoffed at the high rollers who thought they were hot stuff for betting ten grand a hand. That was nothing. She and Tom were the real high rollers. They were betting everything on love at first sight, and they were going to win.

Then Helen's alarm went off, and she rolled over and blinked at the ceiling of a modestly sized bedroom in a government house on an army post, and she remembered everything.

Tom was a little late to the counseling session, but that wasn't why he jogged to get into the building more quickly. It was because he couldn't wait to see his wife again after last night. She couldn't jump ahead on the timeline, but he could move back. They were going to start dating.

He kissed her cheek lightly when he walked into the room with the Tiffany lamp and then he sat directly across from her, knee to knee.

Jennifer asked them how their holiday had gone. They laughed and said, "Very well."

"Today, we're going to try something just a little different with the questions. I think you should each write a question, at least one. Here are the blank cards. I'll give you a moment."

Tom knew he was smiling like a lovesick fool as

he wrote out his questions. *Would you like to have a cup of coffee with me sometime? Can I take you to a movie this weekend?*

Helen scribbled away at her own.

"Finished?" Jennifer asked. "Excellent. Now the twist is, I want you to exchange cards. You won't be asking the questions you wrote. You'll be answering them."

Tom shrugged and traded cards with Helen.

She picked up his card. "Would you like to have a cup of coffee with me sometime?"

"Yes, I would." He picked up the card she'd written. "What was the very first thing I ever bought for you?"

Odd question. He raised one eyebrow as he looked at her.

She smiled. "Vanilla ice cream."

His heart stopped.

"Go ahead and read all your cards, Tom," Jennifer suggested in her politely interested voice.

He drew the next card. "What color bathing suit was I wearing at lunch... *Helen*."

"Red. Bright red, like a lifeguard's. You should have been on *Baywatch*. Hurry up. Read the last one."

His hands were shaking so badly he could barely read what she'd written. "Why was the hem of your wedding gown wet when you ran out of the hotel room with a croissant in your hand?"

"Because after the ceremony, I was so happy I'd married you, I stood in the middle of the fountain in the hotel and told the whole world."

"Helen." Tom vaulted out of his chair and scooped his wife up in his arms and kissed her, oh God, how he kissed her.

"But you're still taking me to the movie on Saturday, right?" she asked him. She was laughing, and she was crying, and damn it, he was crying, too.

He'd thought his wedding day had been the happiest day of his life, but he'd been wrong. This day was.

The marriage counselor left the room. She was no longer needed.

Epilogue

On Valentine's Day, the 89th Military Police Brigade at Fort Hood, Texas, hosted a very traditional military dinner. The proper order of events was followed. All the traditional toasts were made.

Captain Tom Cross wore the blue evening mess uniform, as did Captain Helen Pallas. Her floor-length blue skirt and her sharp tuxedo-like jacket could not be worn with flowers, but she was seated at a table that had been sprinkled with rose petals. It was the only table in the banquet hall to have such an untra-ditional decoration.

Colonel Oscar Reed stood to close the ceremonies and to open the dance floor. "Ladies and gentlemen, there is one more toast to be made, one that isn't on the official program. Captain Cross, if you will do the honors?"

Tom held the microphone in one hand and a glass of champagne in the other. "Thank you, sir. I know the rumors have been circulating at various rates of speed over the past twelve weeks or so, and tonight, I'd like to lay them to rest. Yes, Captain Pallas and I are married. I'd like to raise a glass in honor of my bride. To Helen Pallas."

"To Helen Pallas," the officers, NCOs and their guests responded with enthusiasm. The sparkle of raised crystal champagne glasses lent just the right atmosphere.

"Thank you," Tom said. "The rumor is also true that we didn't know each other very long before we said our vows. I can only tell you that when you meet the right one, you know, and we didn't hesitate. Maybe it was all of our fine army training that inspired us to seize the opportunity to advance."

He paused until the approving *ooh-rahs* quieted down.

"Some of you in this room, like some of our relatives on both sides, think we should do the whole thing over again with all of our friends and family around." He looked at Helen and remembered everything—and smiled. "But we had a great wedding. We've made our vows, and I wouldn't trade how we did it for anything. There's only one thing we missed. I never got to show off my beautiful bride on the dance floor. We've never had our first dance. So, if you would indulge me…"

He set down his champagne glass and handed the microphone to Colonel Reed. Tom offered Helen his hand. She rose gracefully and looked absolutely smashing, a wife to make a man glad to be alive as he escorted her to the center of the dance floor. He slipped one arm around her back in the properly formal, officially approved, traditional dance hold.

Colonel Reed nodded to signal the start of the music as he addressed the crowd. "And now, ladies and gentlemen, for their first dance together as husband and wife, Tom and his lovely bride, Helen."

The sound of spoons clinking on champagne glasses drowned out the music. Nobody in the ballroom was going to be able to hear the music and dance as long as the crowd kept that up, so Tom decided it was common sense leadership to toss the regulations out the window. The groom kissed his bride. Thoroughly.

They lived happily ever after.

* * * * *

*If you loved this story, look out for
Caro Carson's next book,*

The Majors' Holiday Hideaway

coming in November 2018!

*And for more great military romances, try these
other books in the American Heroes miniseries:*

Special Forces Father
by Victoria Pade

Show Me a Hero
by Allison Leigh

&

The Captain's Baby Bargain
by Merline Lovelace

*available now wherever Harlequin Special Edition
books and ebooks are sold.*

CHAPTER ONE

"THIS IS TOTALLY LAME. Why do we have to stay here and wait for you? We can walk home in, like, ten minutes."

Daniela Capelli drew in a deep breath and prayed for patience, something she seemed to be doing with increasing frequency these days when it came to her thirteen-year-old daughter. "It's starting to snow and already almost dark."

Silver rolled her eyes, something *she* did with increasing frequency these days. "So what? A little snow won't kill us. I would hardly even call that snow. We had way bigger storms than this back in Boston. Remember that big blizzard a few years ago, when school was closed for, like, a week?"

"I remember," her younger daughter, Mia, said, looking up from her coloring book at Dani's desk at the Haven Point Veterinary Clinic. "I stayed home from preschool and I watched Anna and Elsa a thousand times, until you said your eardrums would explode if I played it one more time."

Dani could hear a bark from the front office that likely signaled the arrival of her next client and knew she didn't have time to stand here arguing with an obstinate teenager.

"Mia can't walk as fast as you can. You'll end up frustrated with her and you'll both be freezing before you make it home," she pointed out.

"So she can stay here and wait for you while I walk home. I just told Chelsea we could FaceTime about the new dress she bought and she can only do it for another hour before her dad comes to pick her up for his visitation."

"Why can't you FaceTime here? I only have two more patients to see. I'll be done in less than an hour, then we can all go home together. You can hang out in the waiting room with Mia, where the Wi-Fi signal is better."

Silver gave a huge put-upon sigh but picked up her backpack and stalked out of Dani's office toward the waiting room.

"Can I turn on the TV out there?" Mia asked as she gathered her papers and crayons. "I like the dog shows."

The veterinary clinic showed calming clips of animals on a big flat-screen TV set low to the ground for their clientele.

"After Silver's done with her phone call, okay?"

"She'll take *forever*," Mia predicted with a gloomy look. "She always does when she's talking to Chelsea."

Dani fought to hide a smile. "Thanks for your patience, sweetie, with her and with me. Finish your math worksheet while you're here, then when we get home, you can watch what you want."

Both the Haven Point elementary and middle schools were within walking distance of the clinic and it had become a habit for Silver to walk to the elementary school and then walk with Mia to the clinic to spend a few hours until they could all go home together.

Of late, Silver had started to complain that she didn't want to pick her sister up at the elementary school every day, that she would rather they both just took their respective school buses home, where Silver could watch her sister without having to hang out at the boring veterinary clinic.

This working professional/single mother gig was *hard*, she thought as she ushered Mia to the waiting room. Then again, in most ways it was much easier than the veterinary student/single mother gig had been.

When they entered the comfortable waiting room— with its bright colors, pet-friendly benches and big fish tank—Mia faltered for a moment, then sidestepped behind Dani's back.

She saw instantly what had caused her daughter's nervous reaction. Funny. Dani felt the same way. She wanted to hide behind somebody, too.

The receptionist had given her the files with the dogs' names that were coming in for a checkup but hadn't mentioned their human was Ruben Morales. Her gorgeous next-door neighbor.

Dani's palms instantly itched and her stomach felt

as if she'd accidentally swallowed a flock of butter-flies.

"Deputy Morales," she said, then paused, hating the slightly breathless note in her voice.

What *was* it about the man that always made her so freaking nervous?

He was big, yes, at least six feet tall, with wide shoulders, tough muscles and a firm, don't-mess-with-me jawline.

It wasn't just that. Even without his uniform, the man exuded authority and power, which instantly raised her hackles and left her uneasy, something she found both frustrating and annoying about herself.

No matter how far she had come, how hard she had worked to make a life for her and her girls, she still sometimes felt like the troublesome foster kid from Queens.

She had done her best to avoid him in the months they had been in Haven Point, but that was next to impossible when they lived so close to each other—and when she was the intern in his father's veterinary practice.

"Hey, Doc," he said, flashing her an easy smile she didn't trust for a moment. It never quite reached his dark, long-lashed eyes, at least where she was concerned.

While she might be uncomfortable around Ruben Morales, his dogs were another story.

He held the leashes of both of them, a big, muscular Belgian shepherd and an incongruously paired little Chi-poo, and she reached down to pet both of them. They sniffed her and wagged happily, the big dog's tail nearly knocking over his small friend.

That was the thing she loved most about dogs. They were uncomplicated and generous with their affection, for the most part. They never looked at people with that subtle hint of suspicion, as if trying to uncover all their secrets.

"I wasn't expecting you," she admitted.

"Oh? I made an appointment. The boys both need checkups. Yukon needs his regular hip and eye check and Ollie is due for his shots."

She gave the dogs one more pat before she straightened and faced him, hoping his sharp cop eyes couldn't notice evidence of her accelerated pulse.

"Your father is still here every Monday and Friday afternoons. Maybe you should reschedule with him," she suggested. It was a faint hope, but a girl had to try.

"Why would I do that?"

"Maybe because he's your father and knows your dogs?"

"Dad is an excellent veterinarian. Agreed. But he's also semiretired and wants to be fully retired this time next year. As long as you plan to stick around in Haven Point, we will have to switch vets and start seeing you eventually. I figured we might as well start now."

He was checking her out. Not *her* her, but her skills as a veterinarian.

The implication was clear. She had been here three months, and it had become obvious during that time in their few interactions that Ruben Morales was extremely protective of his family. He had been polite enough when they had met previously, but always with a certain guardedness, as if he was afraid she planned to take the good name his hardworking father had built up over the years for the Haven Point Veterinary

Clinic and drag it through the sludge at the bottom of Lake Haven.

Dani pushed away her instinctive prickly defensiveness, bred out of all those years in foster care when she felt as if she had no one else to count on—compounded by the difficult years after she married Tommy and had Silver, when she *really* had no one else in her corner.

She couldn't afford to offend Ruben. She didn't need his protective wariness to turn into full-on suspicion. With a little digging, Ruben could uncover things about her and her past that would ruin everything for her and her girls here.

She forced a professional smile. "It doesn't matter. Let's go back to a room and take a look at these guys. Girls, I'll be done shortly. Silver, keep an eye on your sister."

Her oldest nodded without looking up from her phone and with an inward sigh, Dani led the way to the largest of the exam rooms.

She stood at the door as he entered the room with the two dogs, then joined him inside and closed it behind her.

The large room seemed to shrink unnaturally and she paused inside for a moment, flustered and wishing she could escape. Dani gave herself a mental shake. She could handle being in the same room with the one man in Haven Point who left her breathless and unsteady.

All she had to do was focus on the reason he was here in the first place. His dogs.

She knelt to their level. "Hey there, guys. Who wants to go first?"

The Malinois wagged his tail again while his

smaller counterpoint sniffed around her shoes, probably picking up the scents of all the other dogs she had seen that day.

"Ollie, I guess you're the winner today."

He yipped, his big ears that stuck straight out from his face quivering with excitement.

He was the funniest-looking dog, quirky and unique, with wisps of fur in odd places, spindly legs and a narrow Chihuahua face. She found him unbearably cute. With that face, she wouldn't ever be able to say no to him if he were hers.

"Can I give him a treat?" She always tried to ask permission first from her clients' humans.

"Only if you want him to be your best friend for life," Ruben said.

Despite her nerves, his deadpan voice sparked a smile, which widened when she gave the little dog one of the treats she always carried in the pocket of her lab coat. He slurped it up in one bite, then sat with a resigned sort of patience during the examination.

She was aware of Ruben watching her as she carefully examined the dog, but Dani did her best not to let his scrutiny fluster her.

She knew what she was doing, she reminded herself. She had worked so hard to be here, sacrificing all her time, energy and resources of the last decade to nothing else but her girls and her studies.

"Everything looks good," she said after checking out the dog and finding nothing unusual. "He seems like a healthy little guy. It says here he's about six or seven. So you haven't had him from birth?"

"No. Only about two years. He was a stray I picked up off the side of the road between here and Shelter

Springs when I was on patrol one day. He was in a bad way, half-starved, fur matted. As small as he is, it's a wonder he wasn't picked off by a coyote or even one of the bigger hawks. He just needed a little TLC."

"You couldn't find his owner?"

"We ran ads and Dad checked with all his contacts at shelters and veterinary clinics from here to Boise with no luck. I had been fostering him while we looked, and to be honest, I kind of lost my heart to the little guy, and by then Yukon adored him so we decided to keep him."

She was such a sucker for animal lovers, especially those who rescued the vulnerable and lost ones.

And, no, she didn't need counseling to point out the parallels to her own life.

Regardless, she couldn't let herself be drawn to Ruben and risk doing something foolish. She had too much to lose here in Haven Point.

"What about Yukon here?" She knelt down to examine the bigger dog. In her experience, sometimes bigger dogs didn't like to be lifted and she wasn't sure if the beautiful Malinois fell into that category.

Ruben shrugged as he scooped Ollie onto his lap to keep the little Chi-poo from swooping in and stealing the treat she held out for the bigger dog. "You could say he was a rescue, too."

"Oh?"

"He was a K-9 officer down in Mountain Home. After his handler was killed in the line of duty, I guess he kind of went into a canine version of depression and wouldn't work with anyone else. I know that probably sounds crazy."

She scratched the dog's ears, touched by the bond

that could build between handler and dog. "Not at all," she said briskly. "I've seen many dogs go into decline when their owners die. It's not uncommon."

"For a year or so, they tried to match him up with other officers, but things never quite gelled, for one reason or another, then his eyes started going. His previous handler who died was a good buddy of mine from the academy, and I couldn't let him go just anywhere."

"Retired police dogs don't always do well in civilian life. They can be aggressive with other dogs and sometimes people. Have you had any problems with that?"

"Not with Yukon. He's friendly. Aren't you, buddy? You're a good boy."

Dani could swear the dog grinned at his owner, his tongue lolling out.

Yukon was patient while she looked him over, especially as she maintained a steady supply of treats.

When she finished, she gave the dog a pat and stood. "Can I take a look at Ollie's ears one more time?"

"Sure. Help yourself."

He held the dog out and she reached for Ollie. As she did, the dog wriggled a little, and Dani's hands ended up brushing Ruben's chest. She froze at the accidental contact, a shiver rippling down her spine. She pinned her reaction on the undeniable fact that it had been entirely too long since she had touched a man, even accidentally.

She had to cut out this *fascination* or whatever it was immediately. Clean-cut, muscular cops were *not* her type, and the sooner she remembered that the better.

She focused on checking the ears of the little dog, gave him one more scratch and handed him back to Ruben. "That should do it. A clean bill of health. You obviously take good care of them."

He patted both dogs with an affectionate smile that did nothing to ease her nerves.

"My dad taught me well. I spent most of my youth helping out here at the clinic—cleaning cages, brushing coats, walking the occasional overnight boarder. Whatever grunt work he needed. He made all of us help."

"I can think of worse ways to earn a dime," she said.

The chance to work with animals would have been a dream opportunity for her, back when she had few bright spots in her world.

"So can I. I always loved animals."

She had to wonder why he didn't follow in his father's footsteps and become a vet. If he had, she probably wouldn't be here right now, as Frank Morales probably would have handed down his thriving practice to his own progeny.

Not that it was any of her business. Ruben certainly could follow any career path he wanted—as long as that path took him far away from her.

"Give me a moment to grab those medications and I'll be right back."

"No rush."

Out in the hall, she closed the door behind her and drew in a deep breath.

Get a grip, she chided herself. *He's just a hot-looking dude. Heaven knows you've had more than enough experience with those to last a lifetime.*

She went to the well-stocked medication dispensary, found what she needed and returned to the exam room.

Outside the door, she paused for only a moment to gather her composure before pushing it open. "Here are the pills for Ollie's nerves and a refill for Yukon's eye drops," she said briskly. "Let me know if you have any questions—though if you do, you can certainly ask your father."

"Thanks." As he took them from her, his hands brushed hers again and sent a little spark of awareness shivering through her.

She was probably imagining the way his gaze sharpened, as if he had felt something odd, too.

"I can show you out. We're shorthanded today since the veterinary tech and the receptionist both needed to leave early."

"No problem. That's what I get for scheduling the last appointment of the day—though, again, I spent most of my youth here. I think we can find our way."

"It's fine. I'll show you out." She stood outside the door while he gathered the dogs' leashes, then led the way toward the front office.

AFTER THREE MONTHS, Ruben still couldn't get a bead on Dr. Daniela Capelli.

His next-door neighbor still seemed a complete enigma to him. By all reports from his father, she was a dedicated, earnest new veterinarian with a knack for solving difficult medical mysteries and a willingness to work hard. She seemed like a warm and loving mother, at least from the few times he had seen her interactions with her two girls, the uniquely named teenager Silver—who had, paradoxically, purple hair—and the sweet-as-Christmas-toffee Mia, who was probably about six.

He also couldn't deny she was beautiful, with slender features, striking green eyes, dark, glossy hair and a dusky skin tone that proclaimed her Italian heritage—as if her name didn't do the trick first.

He actually liked the trace of New York accent that slipped into her speech at times. It fitted her somehow, in a way he couldn't explain. Despite that, he couldn't deny that the few times he had interacted with more than a wave in passing, she was brusque, prickly and sometimes downright distant.

His father adored her and wouldn't listen to a negative thing about her.

You just have to get to know her, Frank had said the other night. He apparently didn't see how diligently Dani Capelli worked to keep anyone else from doing just that.

She wasn't unfriendly, only distant. She kept herself to herself. Did Dani have any idea how fascinated the people of Haven Point were with these new arrivals in their midst?

Or maybe that was just him.

As he followed her down the hall in her white lab coat, his dogs behaving themselves for once, Ruben told himself to forget about his stupid attraction to her.

When they walked into the clinic waiting room, they found her two girls there. The older one was texting on her phone while her sister did somersaults around the room.

Dani stopped in the doorway and seemed to swallow an exasperated sound. "Mia, honey, you're going to have dog hair all over you."

"I'm a snowball rolling down the hill," the girl said. "Can't you see me getting bigger and bigger and bigger?"

He could tell the moment the little girl spotted him and his dogs coming into the area behind her mother. She went still and then slowly rose to her feet, features shifting from gleeful to nervous.

Why was she so afraid of him?

"You make a very good snowball," he said, pitching his voice low and calm as his father had taught him to do with all skittish creatures. "I haven't seen anybody somersault that well in a long time."

She moved to her mother's side and buried her face in Dani's white coat—though he didn't miss the way she reached down to pet Ollie on her way.

"Hey again, Silver."

He knew the older girl from the middle school, where he served as the resource officer a few hours a week. He made it a point to learn all the students' names and tried to talk to them individually when he had the chance, in hopes that if they had a problem they would feel comfortable coming to him.

He had the impression that Silver was like her mother in many ways. Reserved, wary, slow to trust. It made him wonder just who had hurt them.

Don't miss Season of Wonder
by RaeAnne Thayne,
available October 2018
wherever HQN books and ebooks are sold!

#2653 THE MAVERICK'S CHRISTMAS TO REMEMBER
Montana Mavericks: The Lonelyhearts Ranch • by Christy Jeffries
Wedding planner Caroline Ruth comes to after a fall off a ladder believing she's engaged to Craig Clifton—but they've never met before! The doctors don't want Caroline getting too upset, so Craig goes along with the charade. But what's a cowboy to do when his fake feelings turn real?

#2654 THE MAJORS' HOLIDAY HIDEAWAY
American Heroes • by Caro Carson
Major India Woods thought house-sitting in Texas would be just another globe-trotting adventure—until her friend's neighbor, Major Aidan Nord, shows up. But their hot holiday fling is interrupted by his two little girls, and India thinks she might have just found her most exciting adventure yet!

#2655 A STONECREEK CHRISTMAS REUNION
Maggie & Griffin • by Michelle Major
Griffin Stone is back in town, this time with a little boy in tow! Can Maggie forgive his disappearing act? And will Stonecreek win over a tech CEO to host their new headquarters? Find out in the anticipated third book of the Maggie & Griffin trilogy!

#2656 AN UNEXPECTED CHRISTMAS BABY
The Daycare Chronicles • by Tara Taylor Quinn
Tamara Owens is supposed to be finding whoever has been stealing from her father's company. But when she meets prime suspect Flint Collins—and his new charge, infant Diamond—she can't bear to pull away, despite her tragic past. Will Flint be able to look past her original investigation to make them a family by Christmas?

#2657 WYOMING CHRISTMAS SURPRISE
The Wyoming Multiples • by Melissa Senate
Moments before walking down the aisle again, Allie Stark finds her presumed-dead husband at her door. Little does he know, he became the father of four babies in his absence! Can this reunited couple make their family work the second time around?

#2658 THE SERGEANT'S CHRISTMAS MISSION
The Brands of Montana • by Joanna Sims
Former army sergeant Shane Brand's life has stalled. When his new landlady, the lovely Rebecca Adams, and her two children move in, he finds he's suddenly ready to change. Now it's his new mission to be the man the single mom deserves, in time to give them all a dose of Christmas joy.

YOU CAN FIND MORE INFORMATION ON UPCOMING HARLEQUIN® TITLES, FREE EXCERPTS AND MORE AT WWW.HARLEQUIN.COM.

HSECNM1018

Get 4 FREE REWARDS!

We'll send you 2 FREE Books
plus 2 FREE Mystery Gifts.

Harlequin® Special Edition books feature heroines finding the balance between their work life and personal life on the way to finding true love.

FREE Value Over **$20**

*Tamara Owens is supposed to be finding the person
stealing from her father. But when she meets prime
suspect Flint Collins—and his new charge, Diamond—
she can't bear to pull away, despite her tragic past.
Will Flint be able to look past her lies to make them a
family by Christmas?*

*Read on for a sneak preview of
the next book in The Daycare Chronicles,
An Unexpected Christmas Baby
by USA TODAY bestselling author Tara Taylor Quinn.*

How hadn't he heard her first knock?

And then she saw the carrier on the chair next to him. He'd
been rocking it.

"What on earth are you doing to that baby?" she exclaimed,
nothing in mind but to rescue the child in obvious distress.

"Damned if I know," he said loudly enough to be heard
over the noise. "I fed her, burped her, changed her. I've done
everything they said to do, but she won't stop crying."

Tamara was already unbuckling the strap that held the
crying infant in her seat. She was so tiny! Couldn't have been
more than a few days old. There were no tears on her cheeks.

"There's nothing poking her. I checked," Collins said,
not interfering as she lifted the baby from the seat, careful to
support the little head.

It wasn't until that warm weight settled against her that
Tamara realized what she'd done. She was holding a baby.
Something she couldn't do.

She was going to pay. With a hellacious nightmare at the
very least.

The baby's cries had stopped as soon as Tamara picked her up.

"What did you do?" Collins was there, practically touching her, he was standing so close.

"Nothing. I picked her up."

"There must've been some problem with the seat, after all…" He'd tossed the infant head support on the desk and was removing the washable cover.

"I'm guessing she just wanted to be held," Tamara said. What the hell was she doing?

Tearless crying generally meant anger, not physical distress.

And why did Flint Collins have a baby in his office?

She had to put the child down. But couldn't until he put the seat back together. The newborn's eyes were closed and she hiccuped and then sighed.

Clenching her lips for a second, Tamara looked away. "Babies need to be held almost as much as they need to be fed," she told him while she tried to understand what was going on.

He was checking the foam beneath the seat cover and the straps, too. He was fairly distraught himself.

Not what she would've predicted from a hard-core businessman possibly stealing from her father.

"Who is she?" she asked, figuring it was best to start at the bottom and work her way up to exposing him for the thief he probably was.

He straightened. Stared at the baby in her arms, his brown eyes softening and yet giving away a hint of what looked like fear at the same time. In that second she wished like hell that her father was wrong and Collins wouldn't turn out to be the one who was stealing from Owens Investments.

Don't miss
An Unexpected Christmas Baby *by Tara Taylor Quinn,*
available November 2018 wherever
Harlequin® Special Edition *books and ebooks are sold.*

www.Harlequin.com

Looking for more satisfying love stories
with community and family at their core?

Check out **Harlequin® Special Edition**
and **Love Inspired®** books!

New books available every month!

CONNECT WITH US AT:

Facebook.com/groups/HarlequinConnection

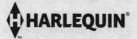 Facebook.com/HarlequinBooks

Twitter.com/HarlequinBooks

Instagram.com/HarlequinBooks

Pinterest.com/HarlequinBooks

ReaderService.com

H HARLEQUIN®

**ROMANCE WHEN
YOU NEED IT**

HFGENRE2018

Looking for inspiration in tales
of hope, faith and heartfelt romance?

Check out **Love Inspired**® and
Love Inspired® **Suspense** books!

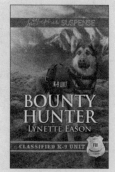

New books available every month!

CONNECT WITH US AT:

Facebook.com/groups/HarlequinConnection

 Facebook.com/HarlequinBooks

Twitter.com/HarlequinBooks

 Instagram.com/HarlequinBooks

Pinterest.com/HarlequinBooks

LIGENRE2018R2